ROBERT LOUIS STEVENSON'S

THE STRANGE CASE OF DR. JEKYLL AND MR. HYDE

A GRAPHIC NOVEL

BY CARL BOWEN &
DANIEL FERRAN

STONE ARCH BOOKS
A CAPSTONE IMPRINT

Graphic Revolve is published by Stone Arch Books
A Capstone Imprint
1710 Roe Crest Drive, North Mankato, Minnesota 56003
www.capstonepub.com

Cataloging-in-Publication Data is available at the Library
of Congress website.
Hardcover ISBN: 978-1-4965-0015-1
Paperback ISBN: 978-1-4965-0034-2

Summary: Scientist Dr. Henry Jekyll believes every
human has two minds: one good and one evil. He
develops a potion to separate them from each other.
Soon, his evil mind takes over, and Dr. Jekyll becomes a
hideous fiend known as Mr. Hyde.

Common Core back matter written by Dr. Katie Monnin.

Color by Sebastian Facio and Daniel Ferran.

Designer: Bob Lentz
Assistant Designer: Peggie Carley
Editor: Donald Lemke
Assistant Editor: Sean Tulien
Creative Director: Heather Kindseth
Editorial Director: Michael Dahl
Publisher: Ashley C. Andersen Zantop

Printed in the United States of America in
Stevens Point, Wisconsin.
052014
008092WZF14

TABLE OF CONTENTS

ABOUT MEDICAL DISCOVERIES

A formula to separate the body's two minds sounds impossible, right? Well, don't be so sure — many of the world's greatest medical advances seemed impossible when they were first discovered.

For hundreds of years, many people feared getting a virus called smallpox. This disease was impossible to cure and often deadly. In the late 1700s, a doctor in England named Edward Jenner noticed that farmers who worked near cattle never got the disease. He believed the farmers had developed an immunity to smallpox because they had been in contact with a similar disease called cowpox. In 1796, Jenner tested his theory. He put a small amount of cowpox into the arm of an eight-year-old boy. The vaccine worked, and the boy never contracted smallpox.

Until the mid-1800s, surgeries to cure injuries or disease were extremely uncommon. The reason was that doctors didn't use anesthesia on their patients. Anesthesia helps prevent pain during an operation. When scientist William T. G. Morton and others discovered these chemicals, doctors and dentists could finally help their patients without hurting them.

Some of the greatest medical discoveries have actually happened by accident. In 1895, scientist Wilhelm Rontgen was performing experiments on cathode rays. During the experiments, he noticed that these rays of electrons could "see through" solid objects. He called them X-rays. Today, X-rays are used to take pictures of bones, teeth, and organs.

Another famous accident happened in 1928. That year, Professor Alexander Fleming left a pile of petri dishes in his laboratory sink. He noticed that mold growing on one of the dishes had killed a bacteria sample. After testing, Fleming discovered the mold was Penicillium notatum. Soon, other scientists would find that penicillin could be used to cure bacterial infections in humans.

Before the 1950s, a disease called poliomyelitis, commonly known as polio, infected thousands of children each year. The disease could cause paralysis and even death. In 1952, Dr. Jonas Salk created a vaccine for the awful disease. Today, children continue to receive the vaccine, and the disease has been nearly wiped out.

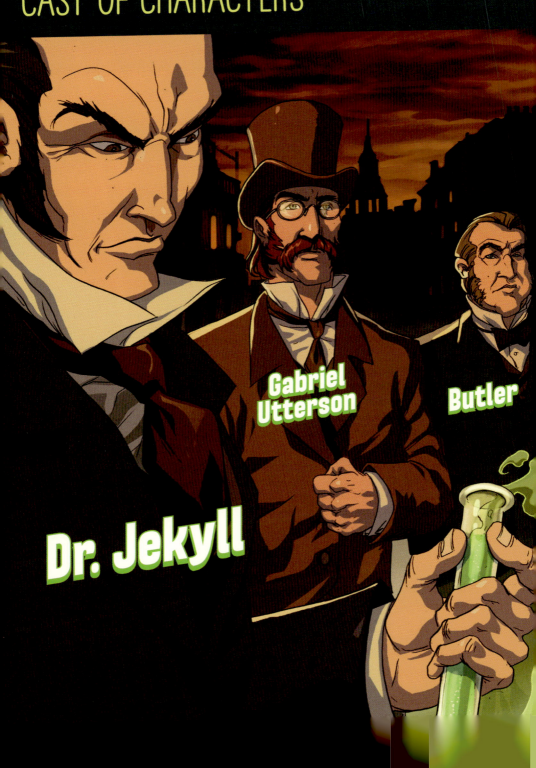

Gabriel Utterson

Butler

Dr. Jekyll

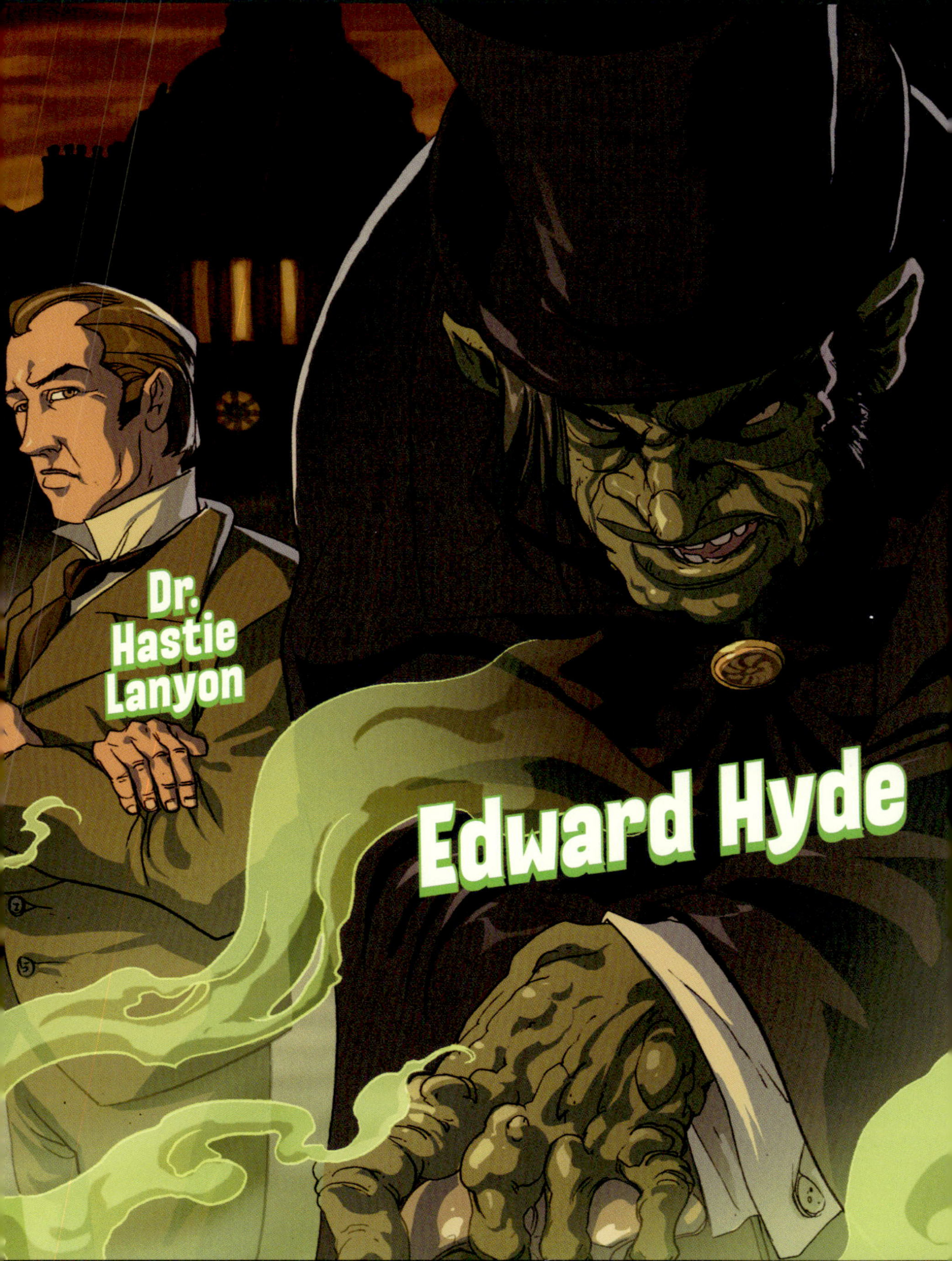
Dr. Hastie Lanyon
Edward Hyde

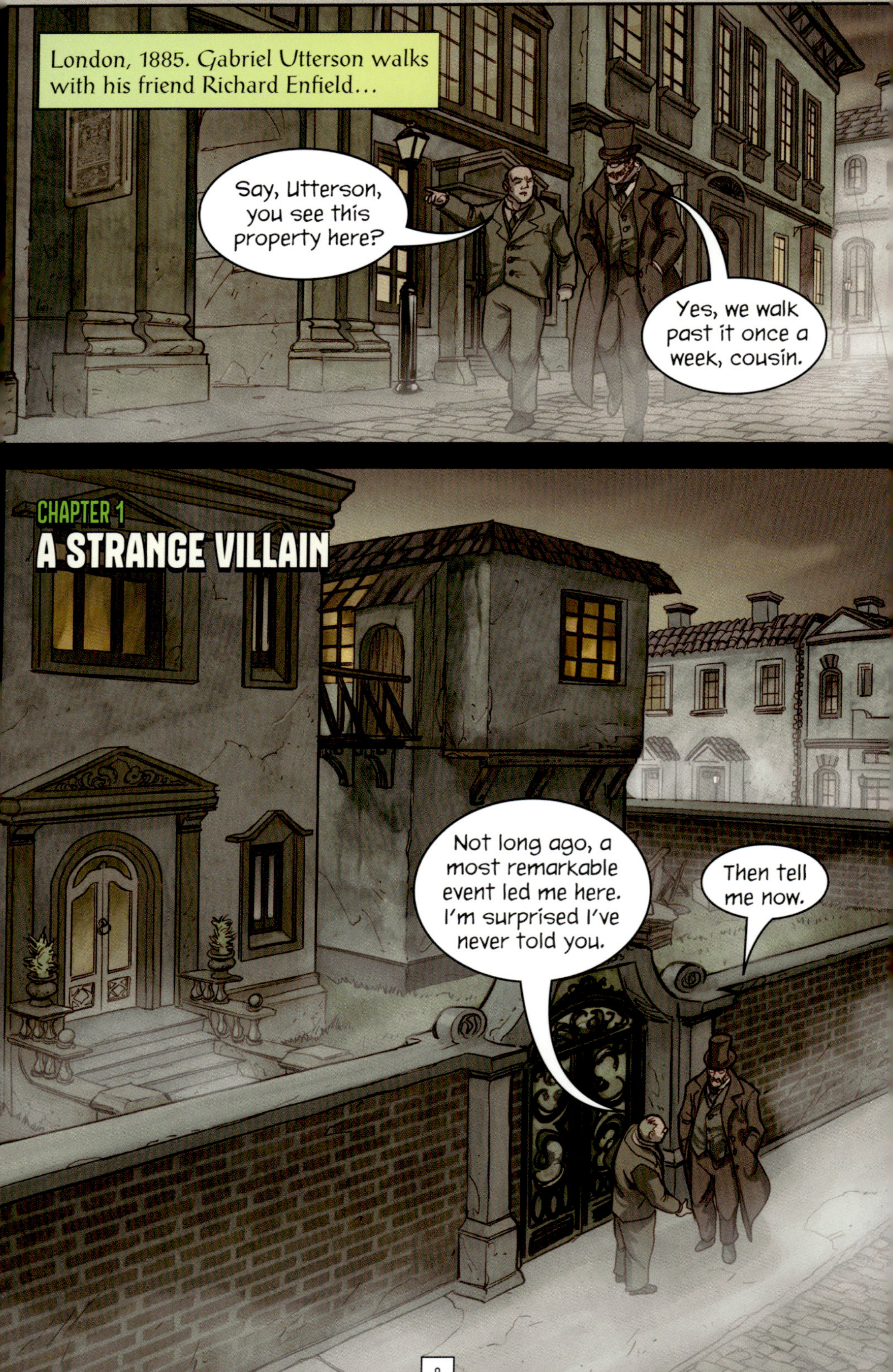
London, 1885. Gabriel Utterson walks with his friend Richard Enfield...
Say, Utterson, you see this property here?
Yes, we walk past it once a week, cousin.
CHAPTER 1
A STRANGE VILLAIN
Not long ago, a most remarkable event led me here. I'm surprised I've never told you.
Then tell me now.

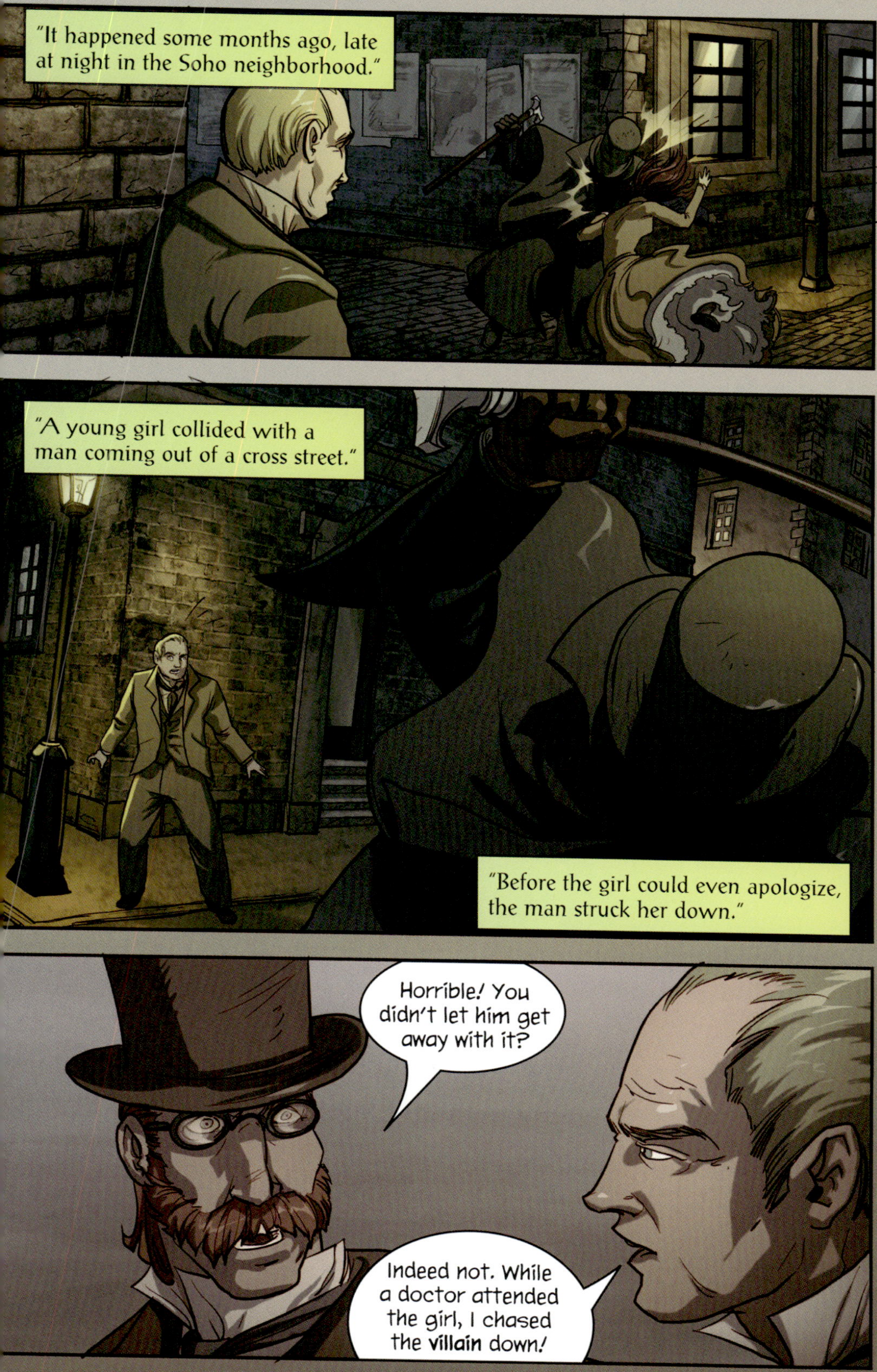
"It happened some months ago, late at night in the Soho neighborhood."
"A young girl collided with a man coming out of a cross street."
"Before the girl could even apologize, the man struck her down."
Horrible! You didn't let him get away with it?
Indeed not. While a doctor attended the girl, I chased the villain down!

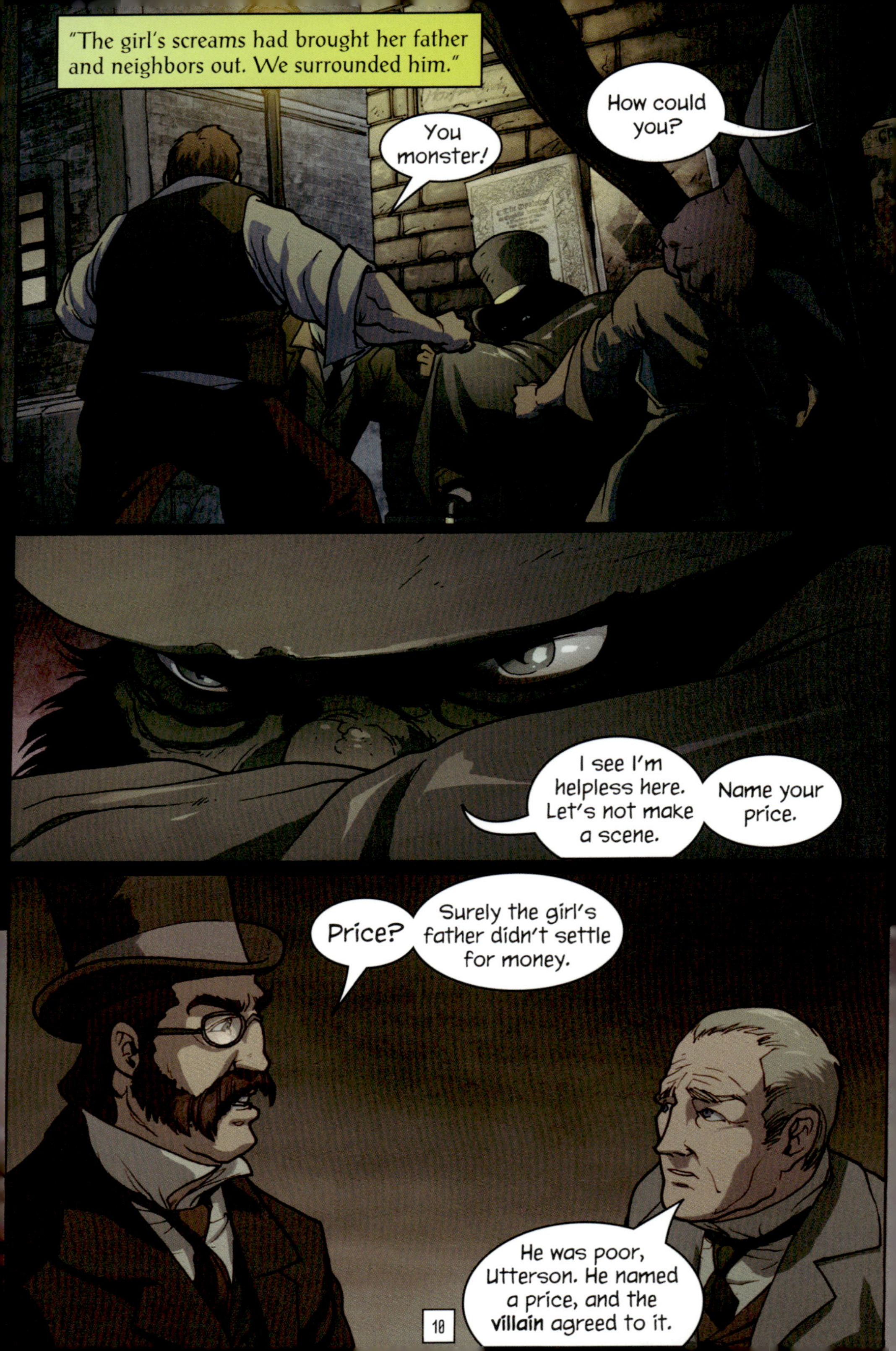
"The girl's screams had brought her father and neighbors out. We surrounded him."
You monster!
How could you?
I see I'm helpless here. Let's not make a scene.
Name your price.
Price?
Surely the girl's father didn't settle for money.
He was poor, Utterson. He named a price, and the **villain** agreed to it.

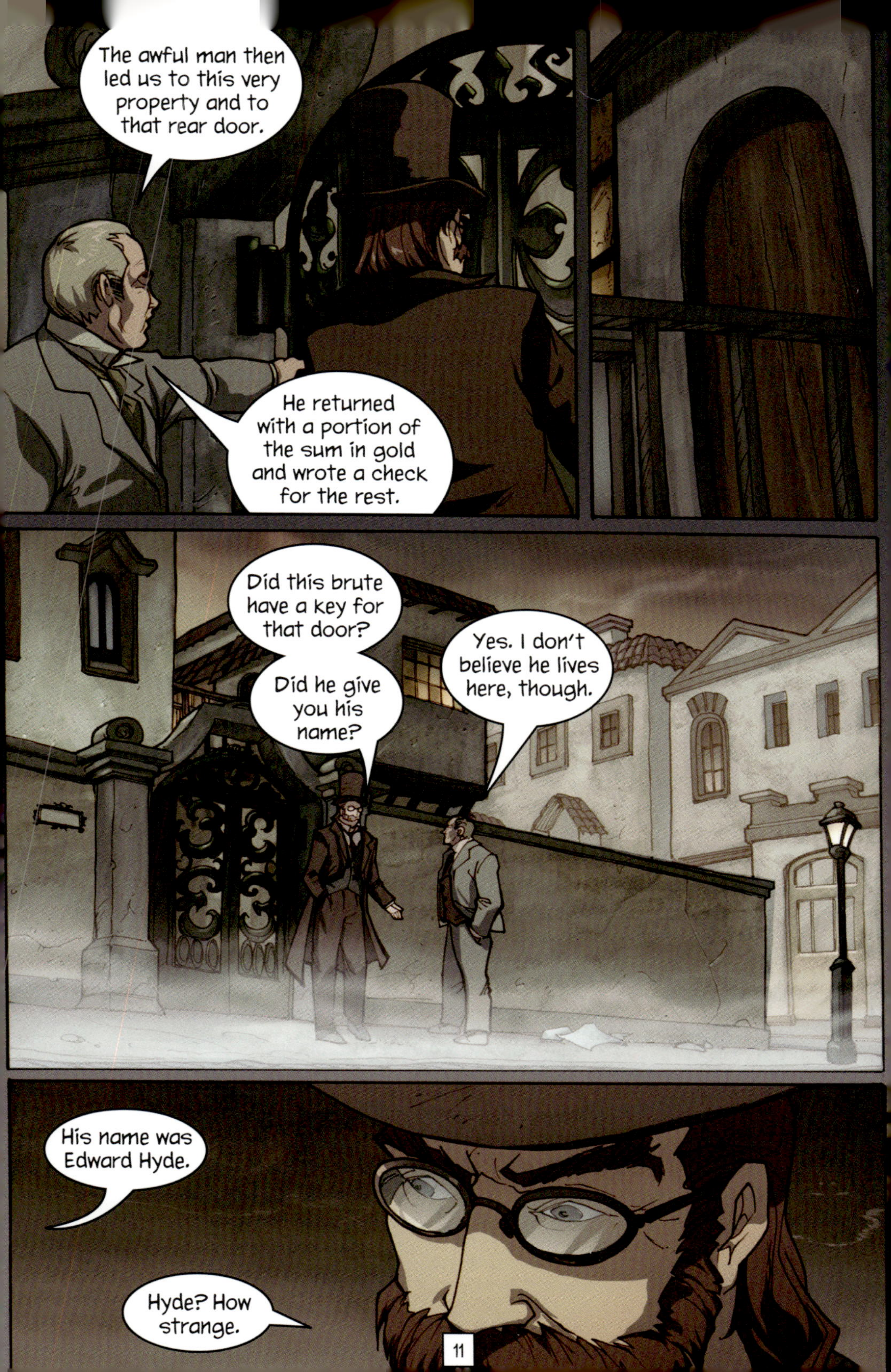
The awful man then led us to this very property and to that rear door.
He returned with a portion of the sum in gold and wrote a check for the rest.
Did this brute have a key for that door?
Did he give you his name?
Yes. I don't believe he lives here, though.
His name was Edward Hyde.
Hyde? How strange.

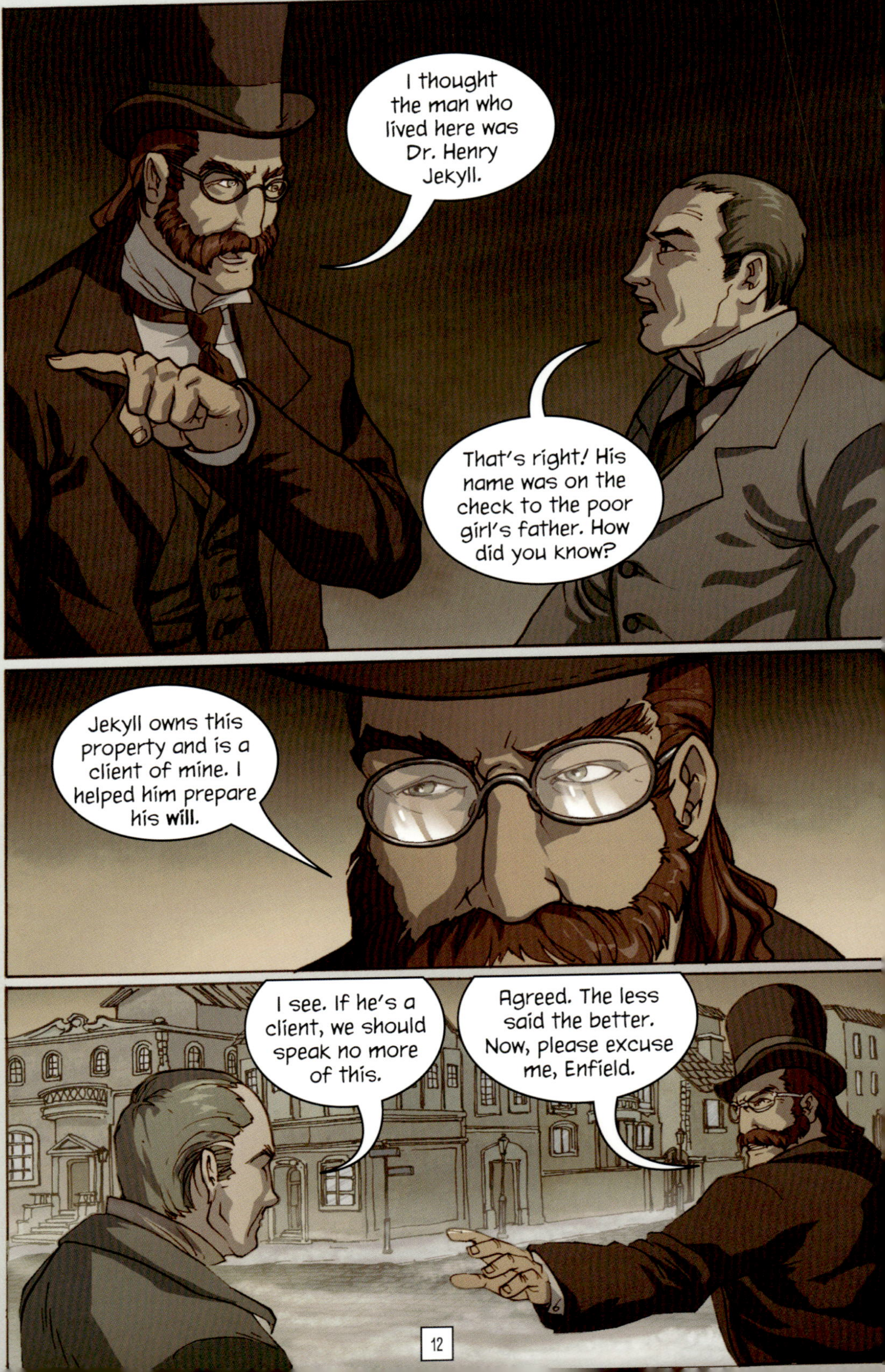
I thought the man who lived here was Dr. Henry Jekyll.
That's right! His name was on the check to the poor girl's father. How did you know?
Jekyll owns this property and is a client of mine. I helped him prepare his **will**.
I see. If he's a client, we should speak no more of this.
Agreed. The less said the better. Now, please excuse me, Enfield.

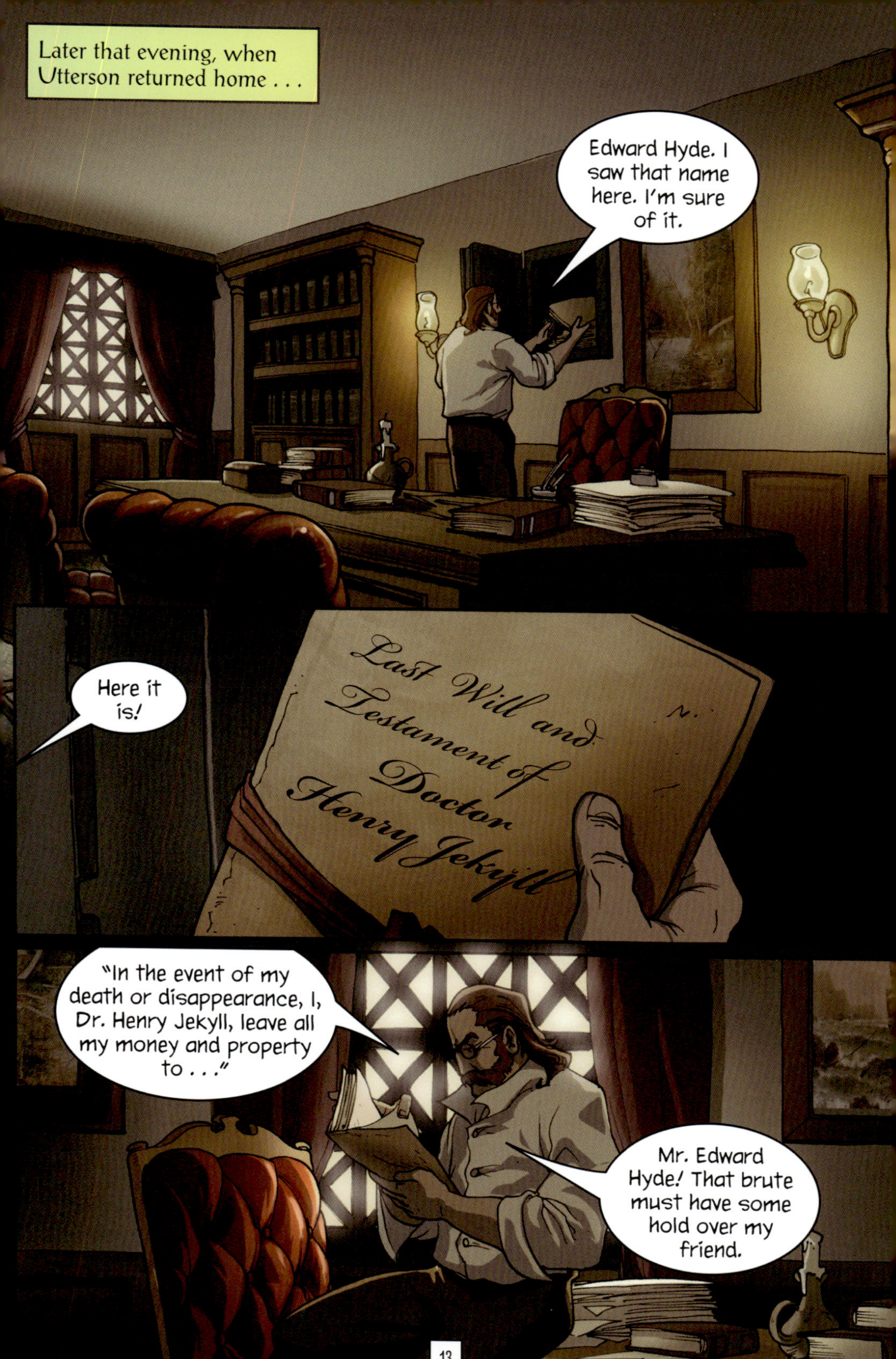
Later that evening, when Utterson returned home . . .
Edward Hyde. I saw that name here. I'm sure of it.
Here it is!
Last Will and Testament of Doctor Henry Jekyll
"In the event of my death or disappearance, I, Dr. Henry Jekyll, leave all my money and property to . . ."
Mr. Edward Hyde! That brute must have some hold over my friend.

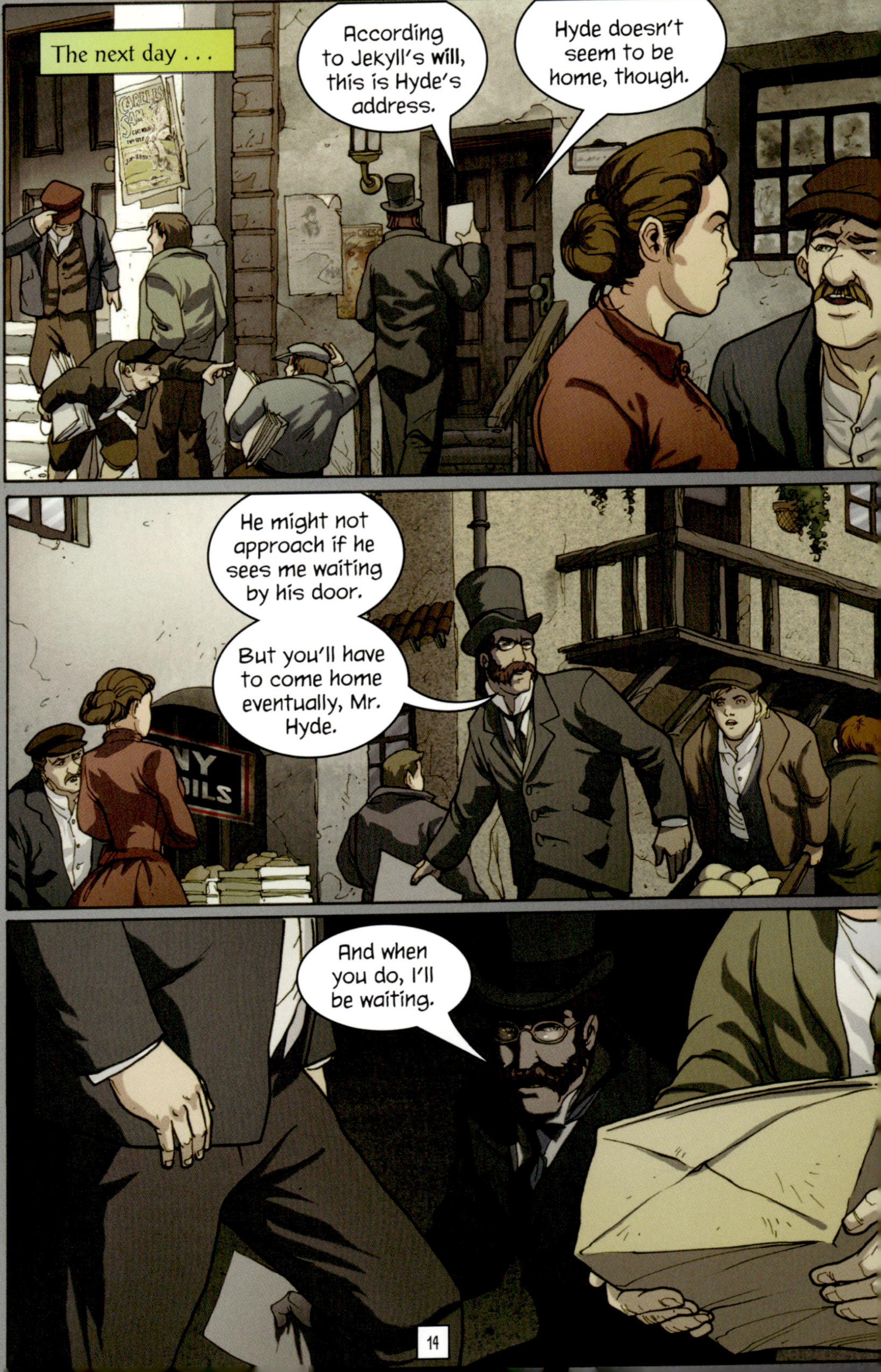
The next day . . .
According to Jekyll's will, this is Hyde's address.
Hyde doesn't seem to be home, though.
He might not approach if he sees me waiting by his door.
But you'll have to come home eventually, Mr. Hyde.
And when you do, I'll be waiting.

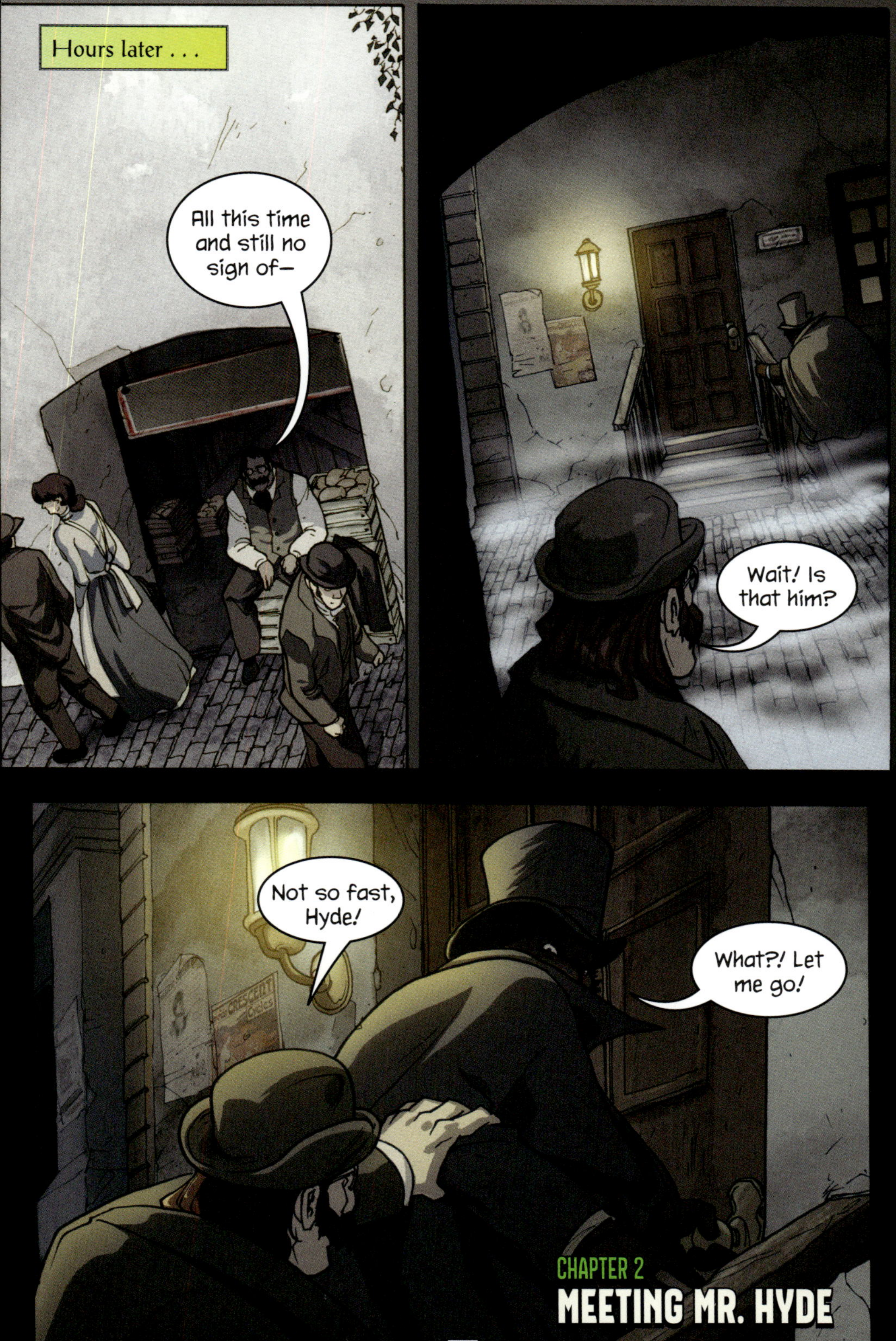
Hours later . . .
All this time and still no sign of–
Wait! Is that him?
Not so fast, Hyde!
What?! Let me go!
CHAPTER 2
MEETING MR. HYDE

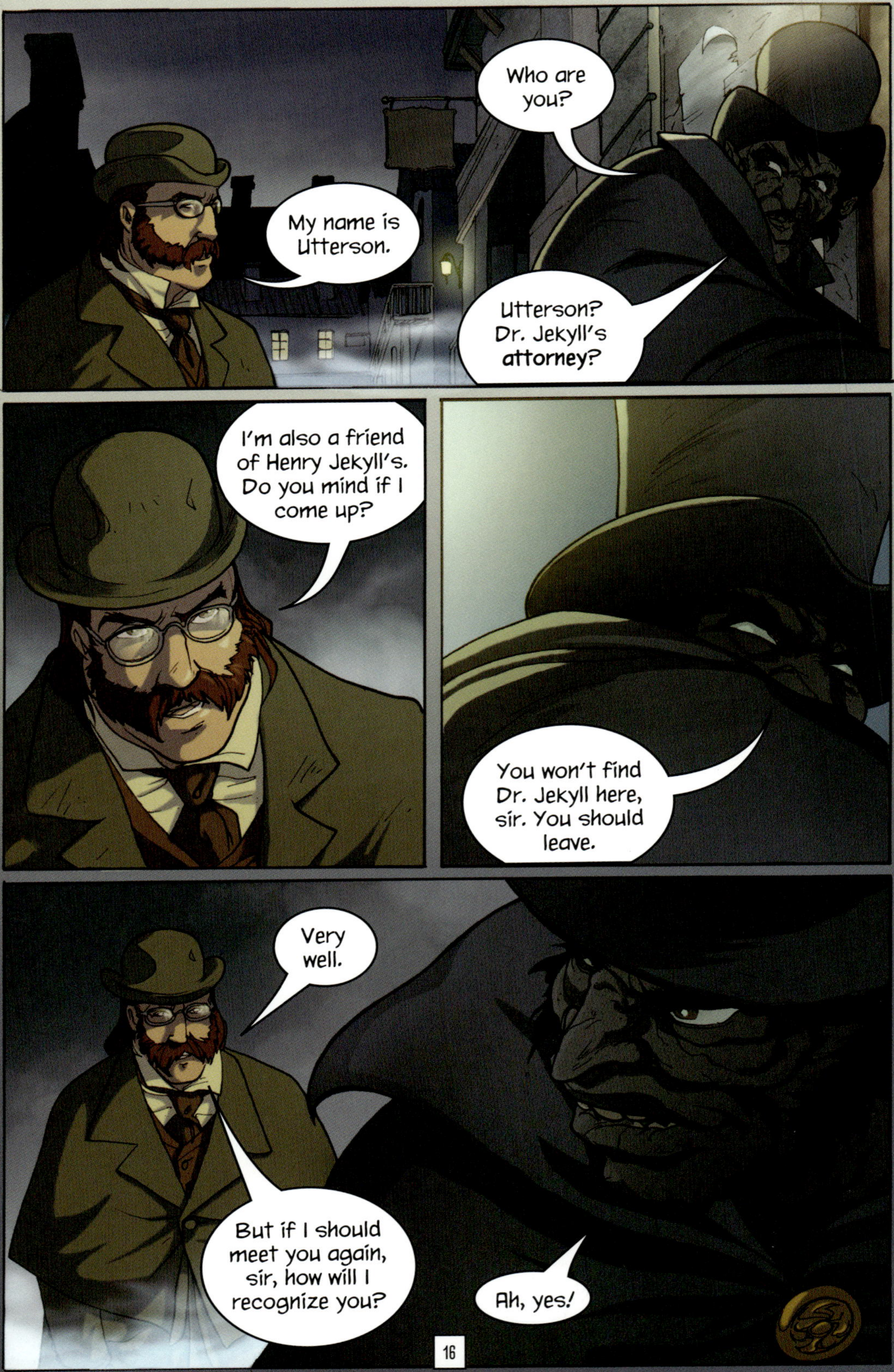
Who are you?
My name is Utterson.
Utterson? Dr. Jekyll's **attorney?**
I'm also a friend of Henry Jekyll's. Do you mind if I come up?
You won't find Dr. Jekyll here, sir. You should leave.
Very well.
But if I should meet you again, sir, how will I recognize you?
Ah, yes!

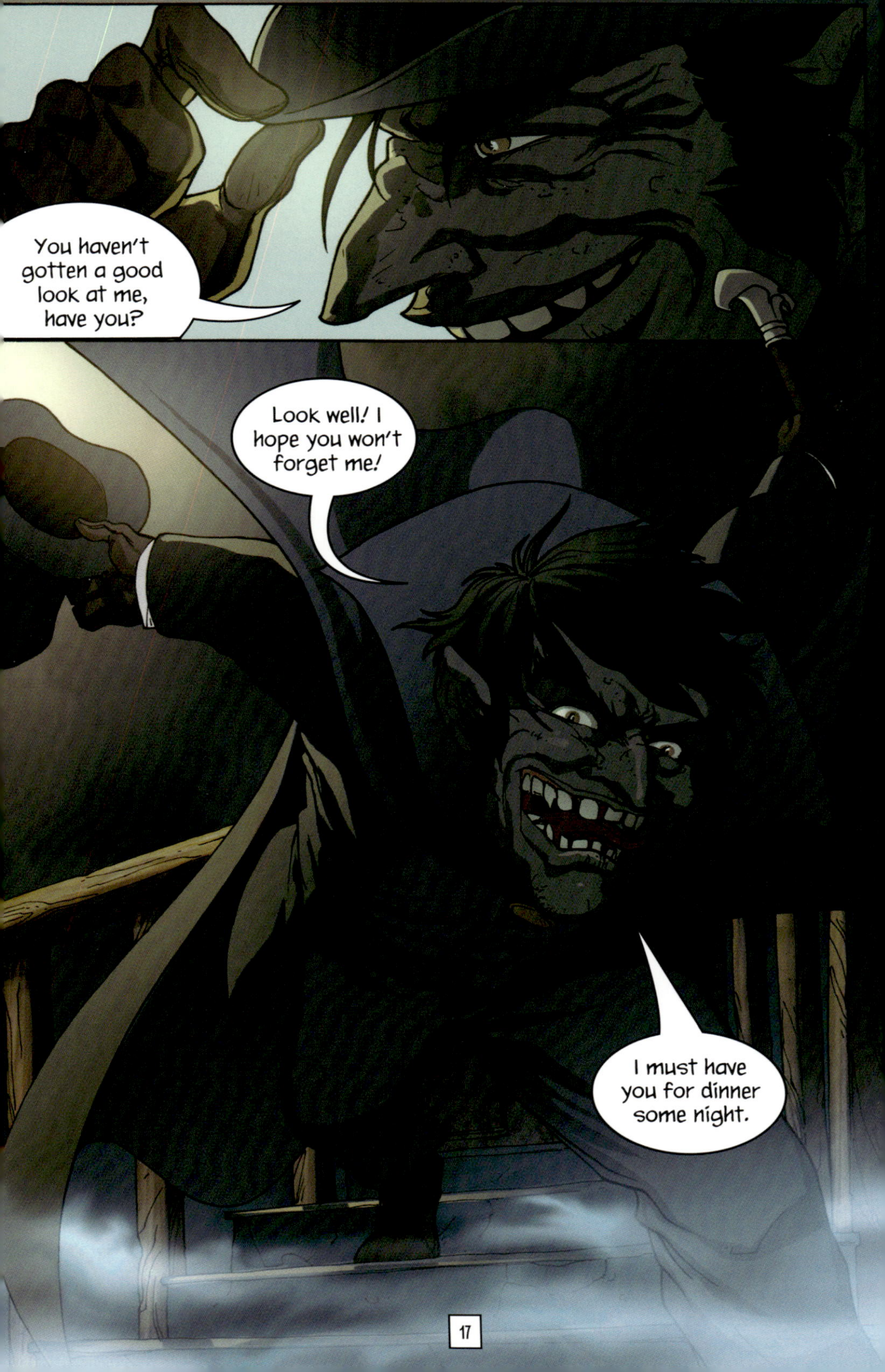
You haven't gotten a good look at me, have you?
Look well! I hope you won't forget me!
I must have you for dinner some night.

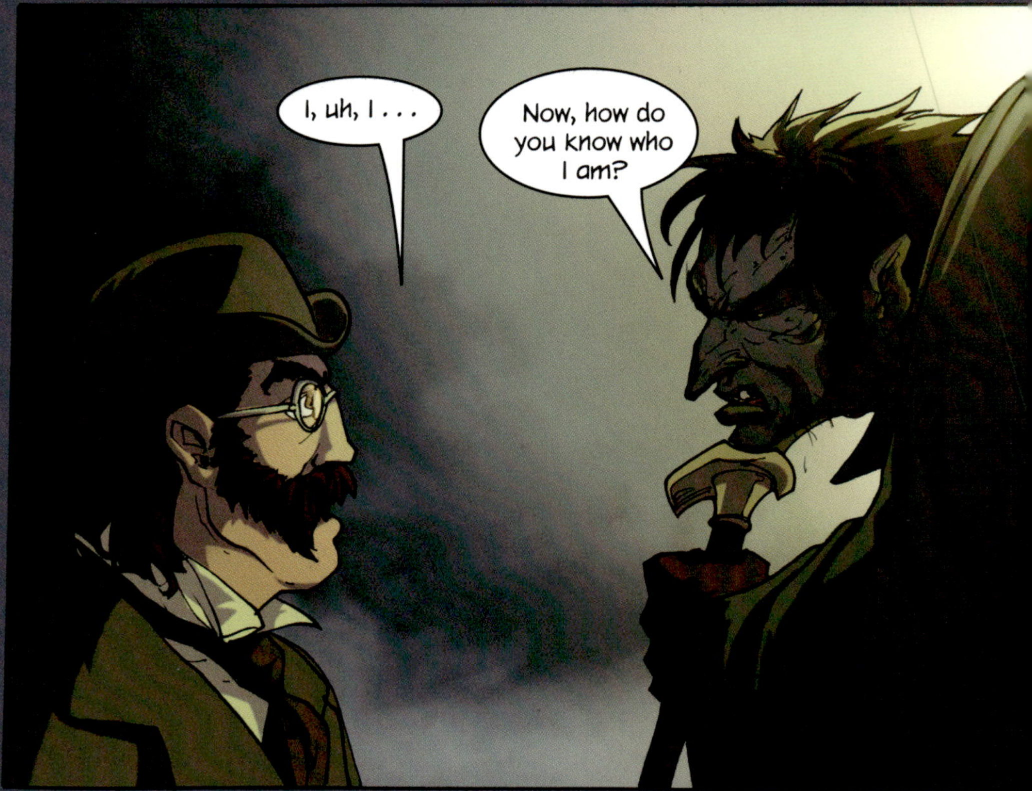
I, uh, I . . .
Now, how do you know who I am?

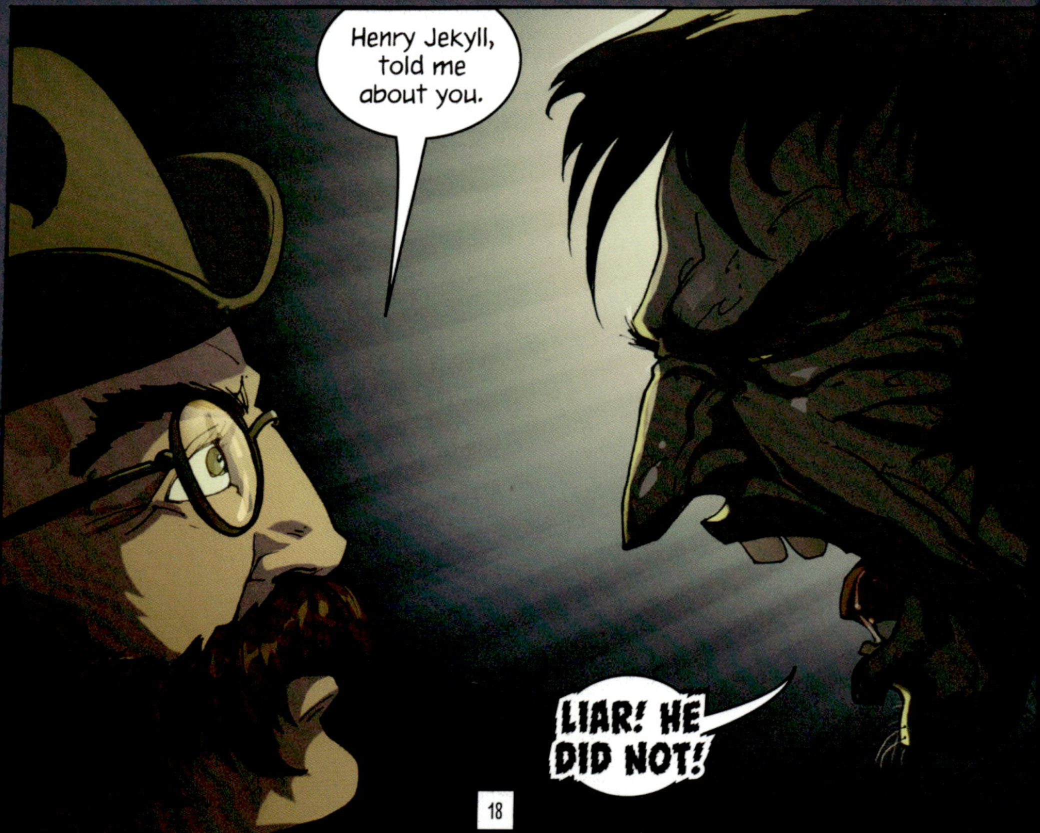
Henry Jekyll, told me about you.
LIAR! HE DID NOT!

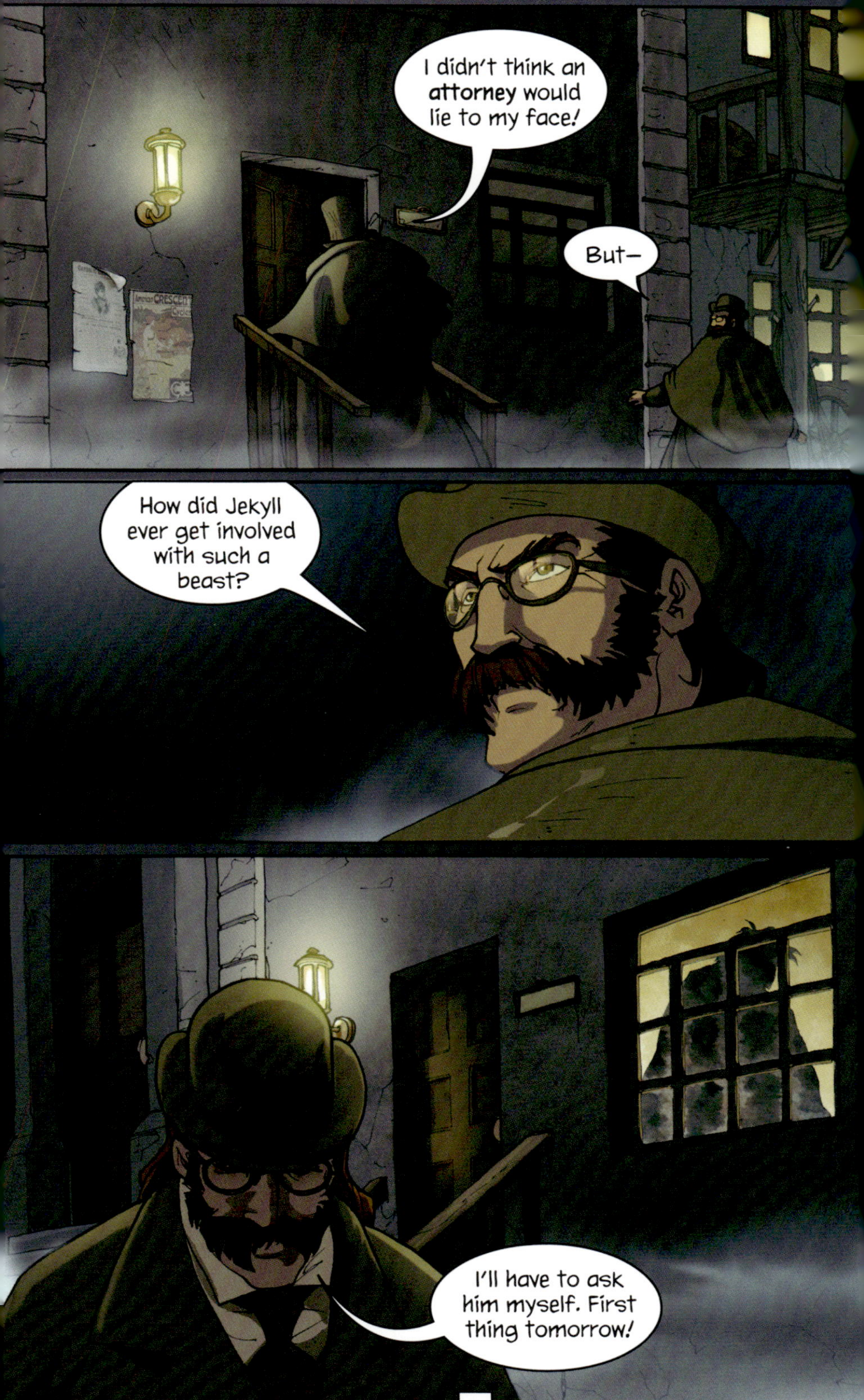
I didn't think an **attorney** would lie to my face!
But–
How did Jekyll ever get involved with such a beast?
I'll have to ask him myself. First thing tomorrow!

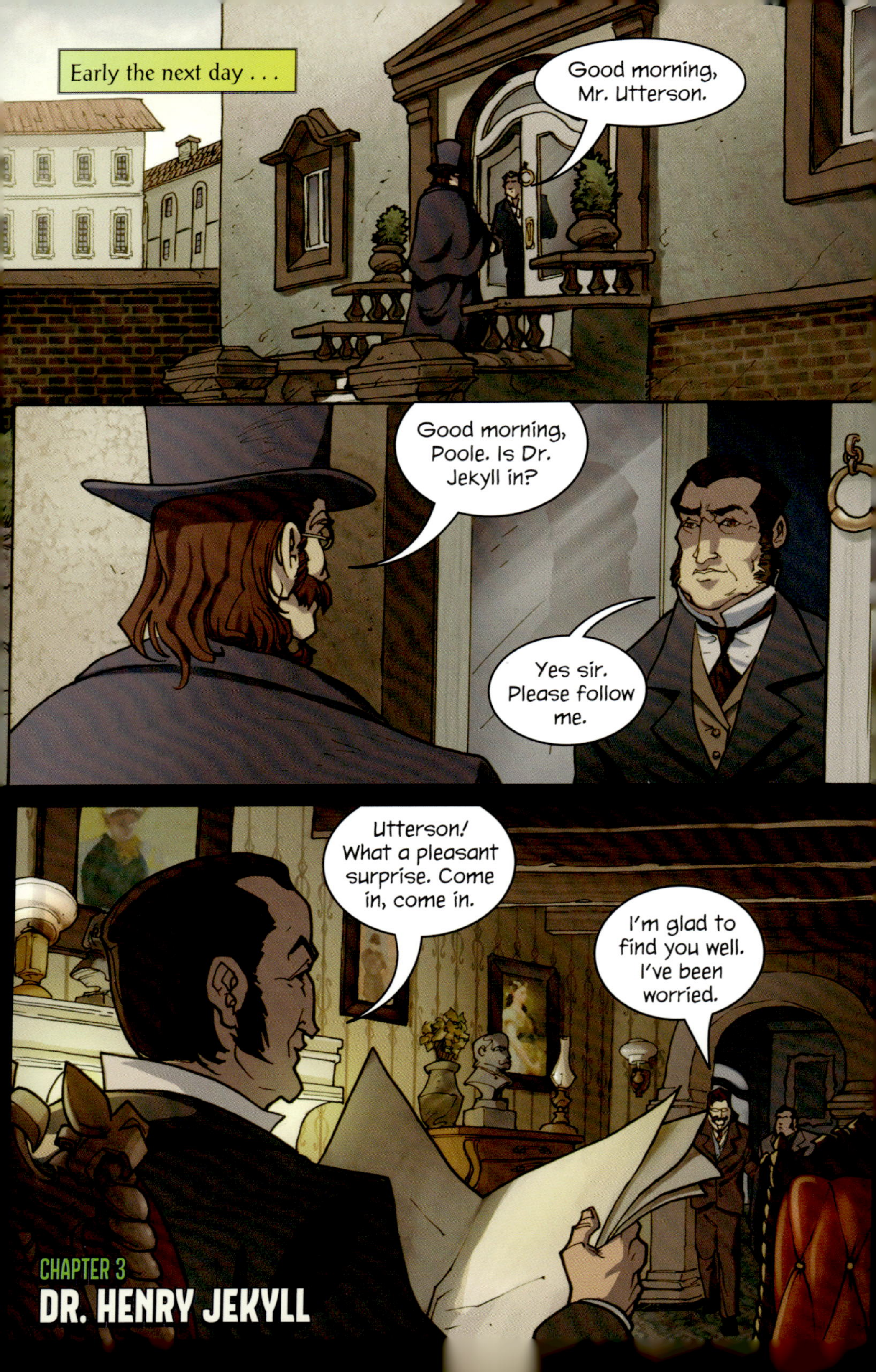
Early the next day . . .
Good morning, Mr. Utterson.
Good morning, Poole. Is Dr. Jekyll in?
Yes sir. Please follow me.
Utterson! What a pleasant surprise. Come in, come in.
I'm glad to find you well. I've been worried.
CHAPTER 3
DR. HENRY JEKYLL

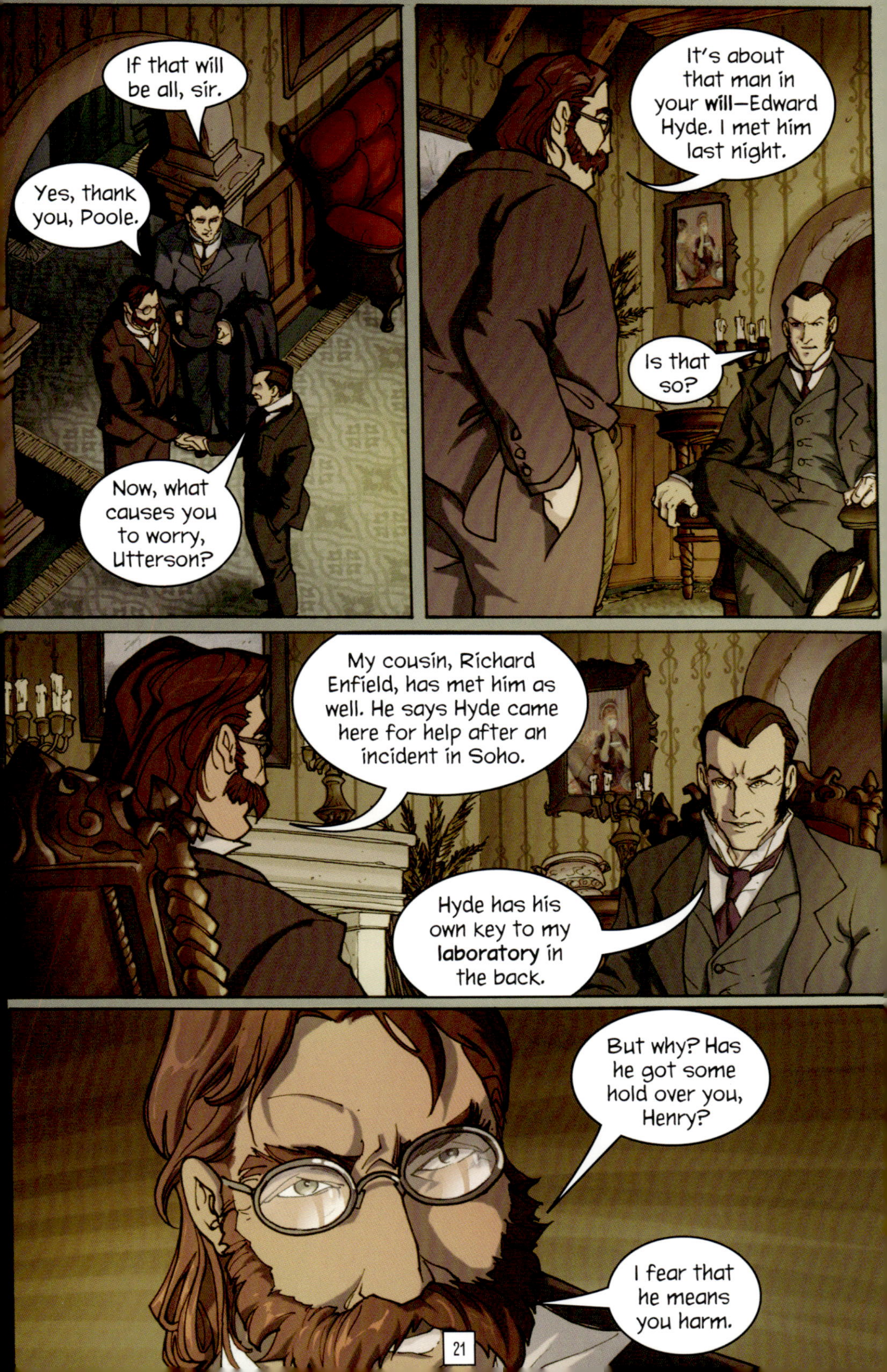
If that will be all, sir.
Yes, thank you, Poole.
Now, what causes you to worry, Utterson?
It's about that man in your will—Edward Hyde. I met him last night.
Is that so?
My cousin, Richard Enfield, has met him as well. He says Hyde came here for help after an incident in Soho.
Hyde has his own key to my laboratory in the back.
But why? Has he got some hold over you, Henry?
I fear that he means you harm.

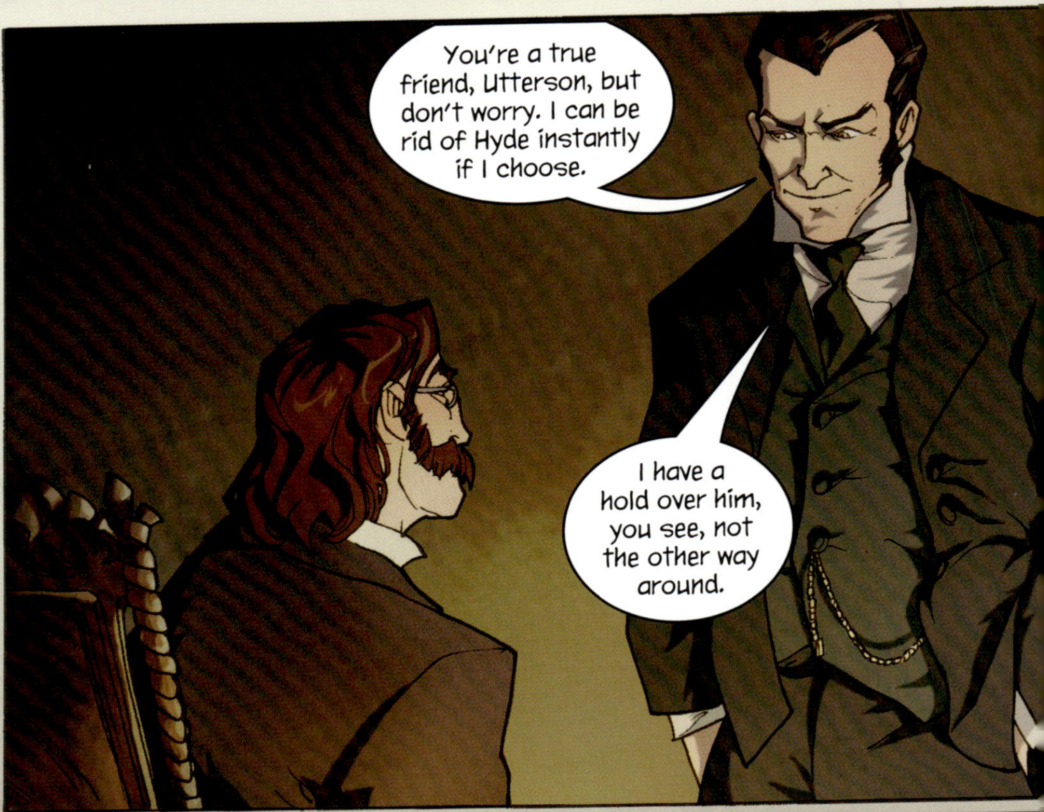
You're a true friend, Utterson, but don't worry. I can be rid of Hyde instantly if I choose.
I have a hold over him, you see, not the other way around.

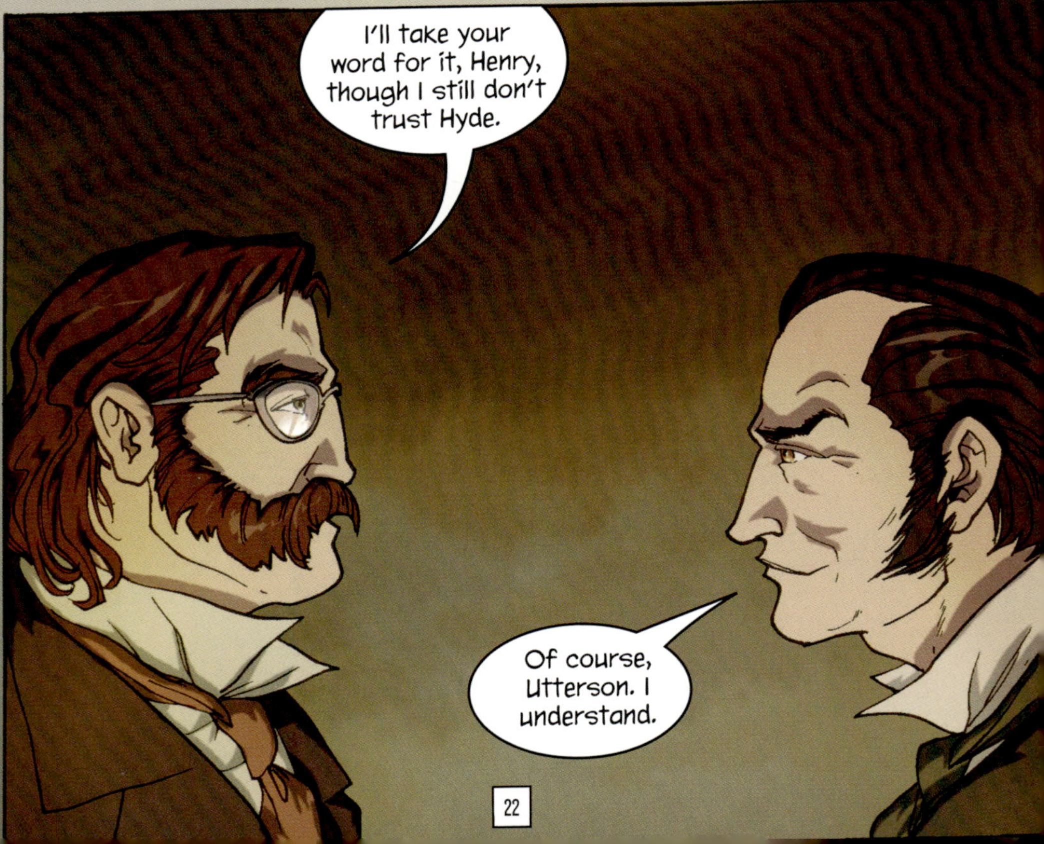
I'll take your word for it, Henry, though I still don't trust Hyde.
Of course, Utterson. I understand.

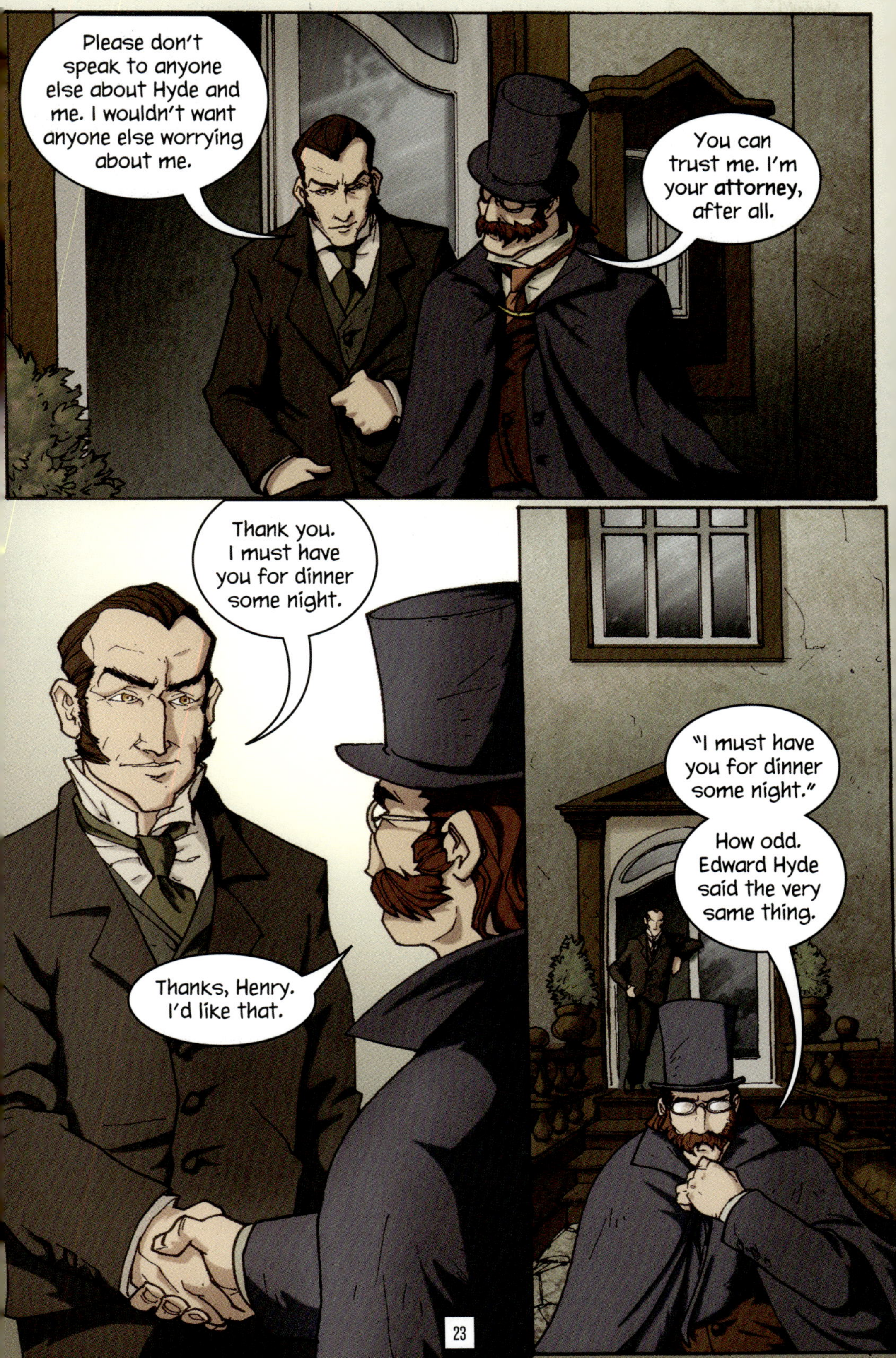
Please don't speak to anyone else about Hyde and me. I wouldn't want anyone else worrying about me.
You can trust me. I'm your **attorney**, after all.
Thank you. I must have you for dinner some night.
Thanks, Henry. I'd like that.
"I must have you for dinner some night."
How odd. Edward Hyde said the very same thing.

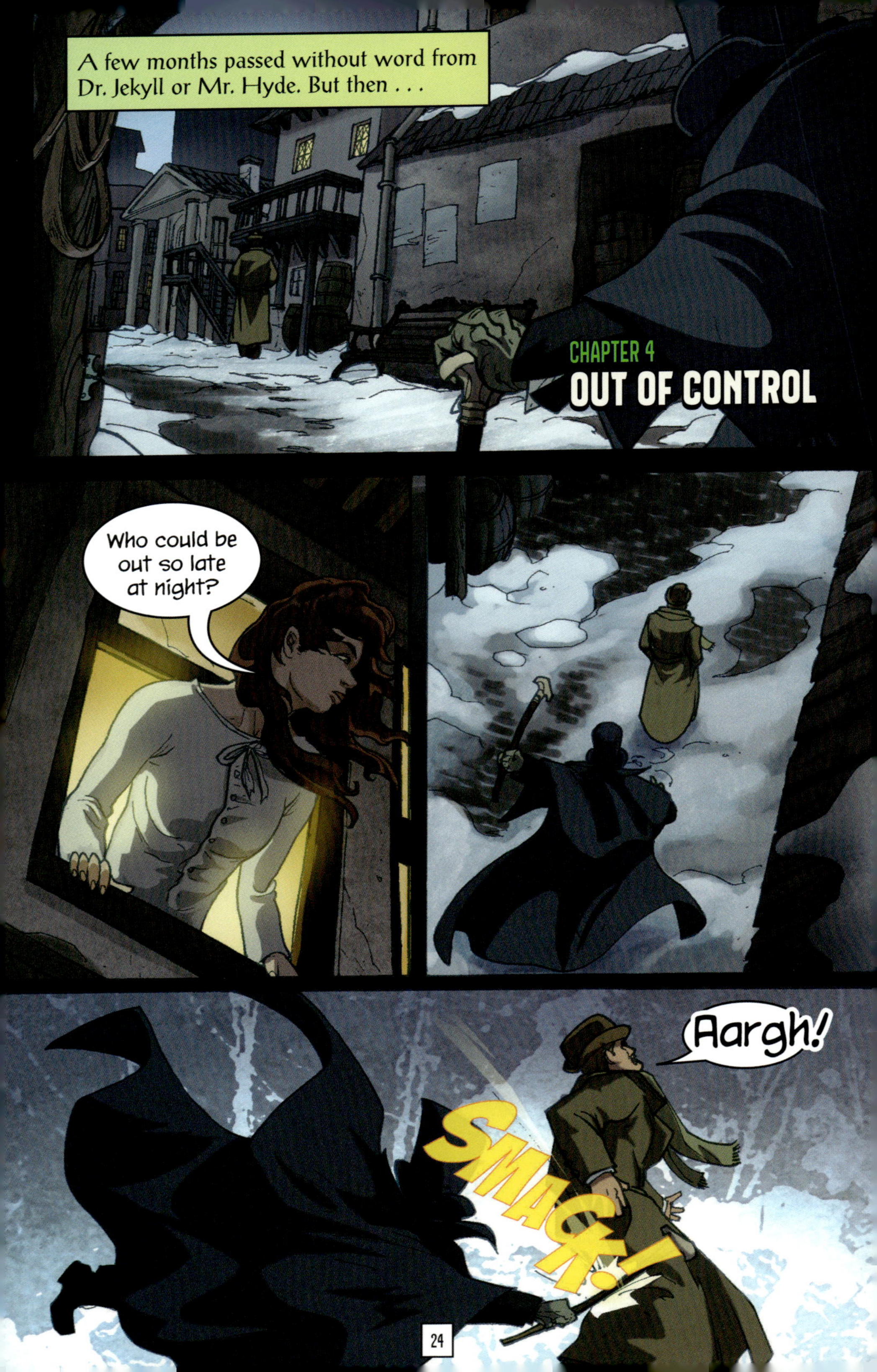
A few months passed without word from Dr. Jekyll or Mr. Hyde. But then . . .
CHAPTER 4
OUT OF CONTROL
Who could be out so late at night?
Aargh!
SMACK!

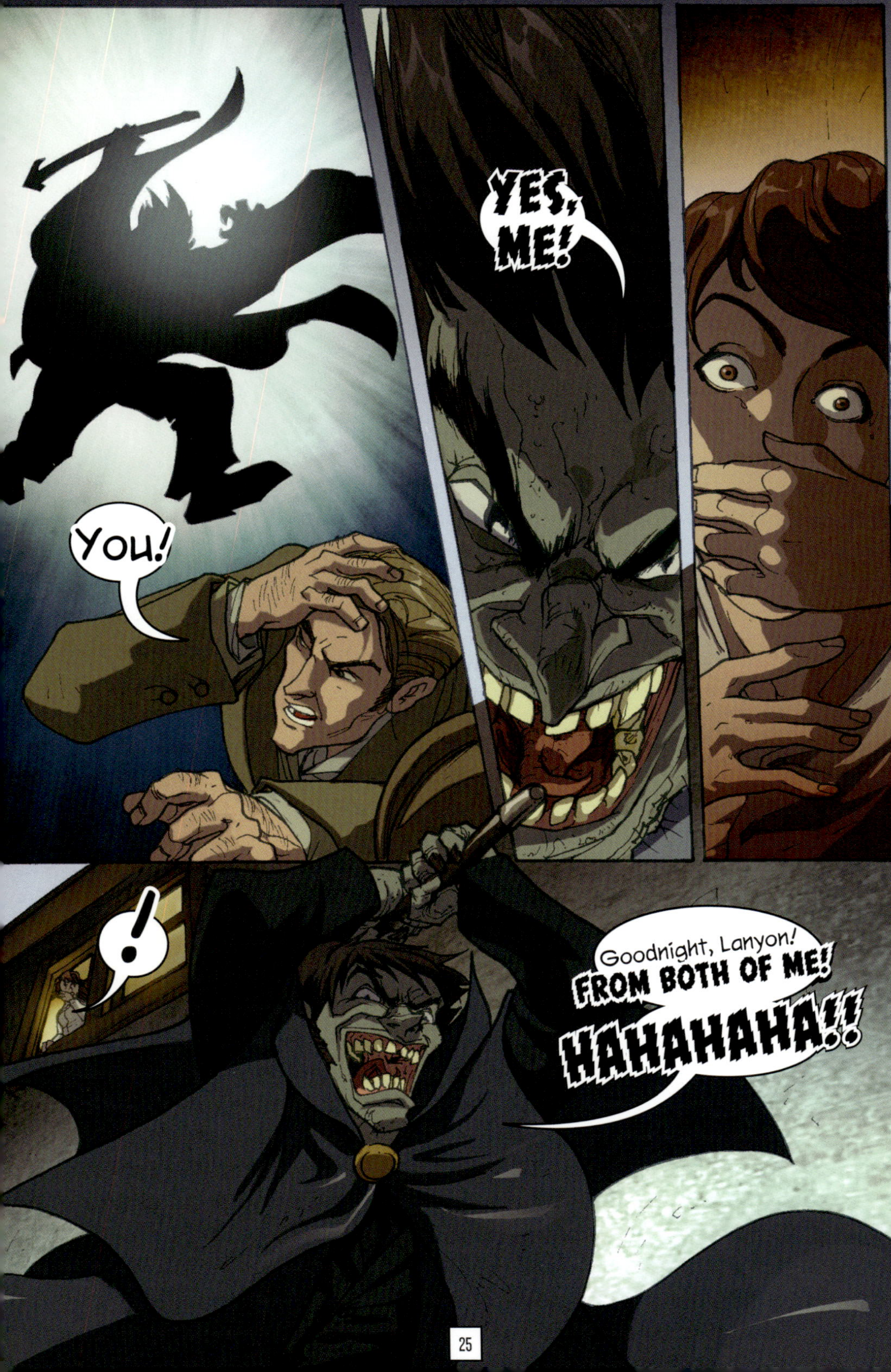
YOU!
YES, ME!
!
Goodnight, Lanyon! FROM BOTH OF ME! HAHAHAHA!!

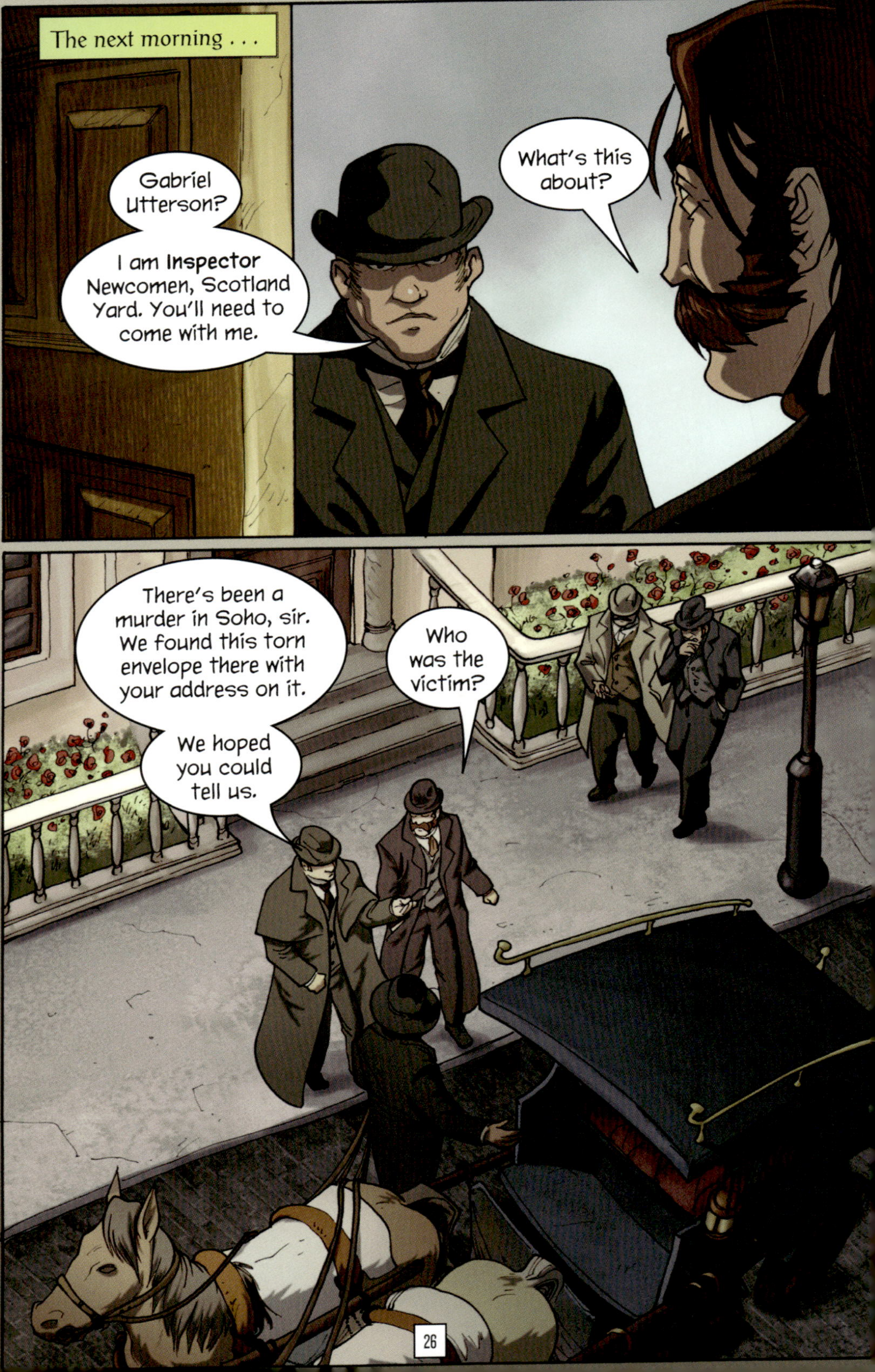
The next morning . . .
Gabriel Utterson?
I am Inspector Newcomen, Scotland Yard. You'll need to come with me.
What's this about?
There's been a murder in Soho, sir. We found this torn envelope there with your address on it.
Who was the victim?
We hoped you could tell us.

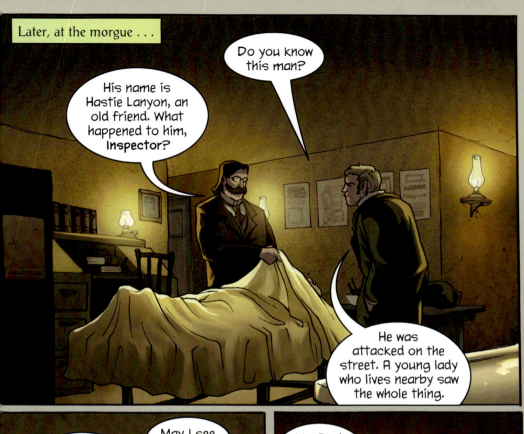

Do you know this man?

His name is Hastie Lanyon, an old friend. What happened to him, Inspector?

He was attacked on the street. A young lady who lives nearby saw the whole thing.

We found this lying in the gutter.

May I see that?

My God, I've seen this before!

I believe I know where the murderer lives!

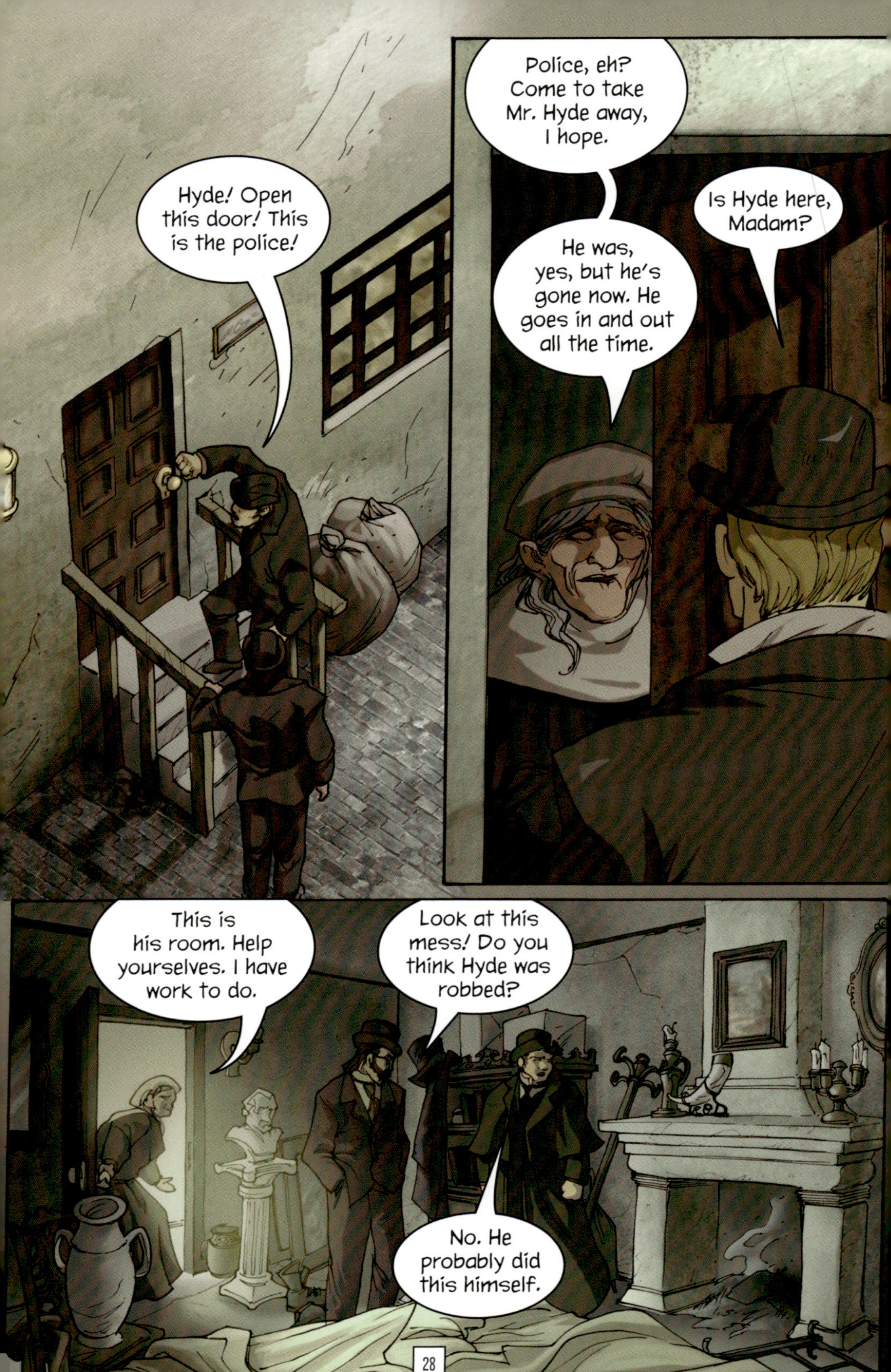
Hyde! Open this door! This is the police!
Police, eh? Come to take Mr. Hyde away, I hope.
Is Hyde here, Madam?
He was, yes, but he's gone now. He goes in and out all the time.
This is his room. Help yourselves. I have work to do.
Look at this mess! Do you think Hyde was robbed?
No. He probably did this himself.

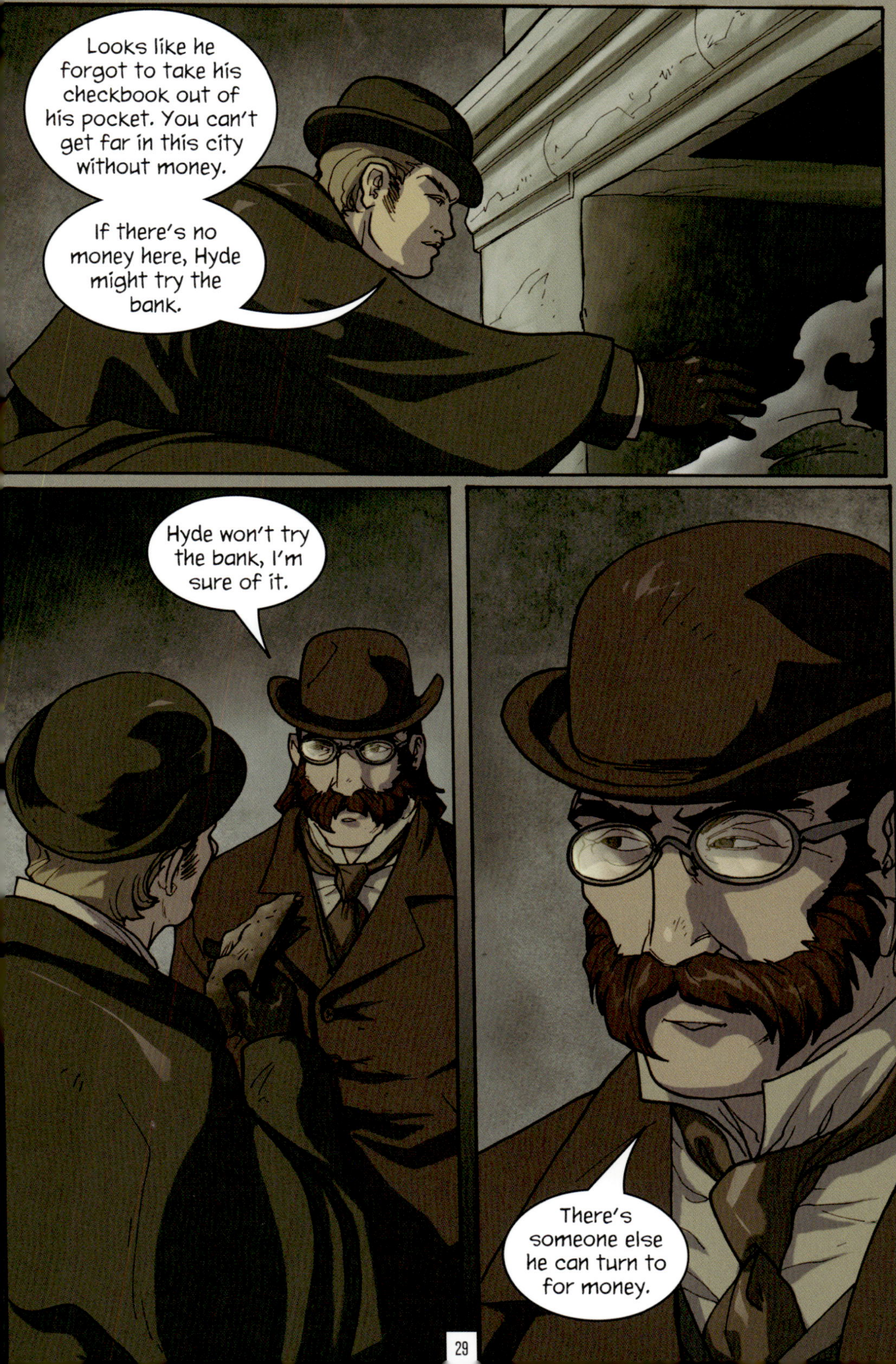
Looks like he forgot to take his checkbook out of his pocket. You can't get far in this city without money.
If there's no money here, Hyde might try the bank.
Hyde won't try the bank, I'm sure of it.
There's someone else he can turn to for money.

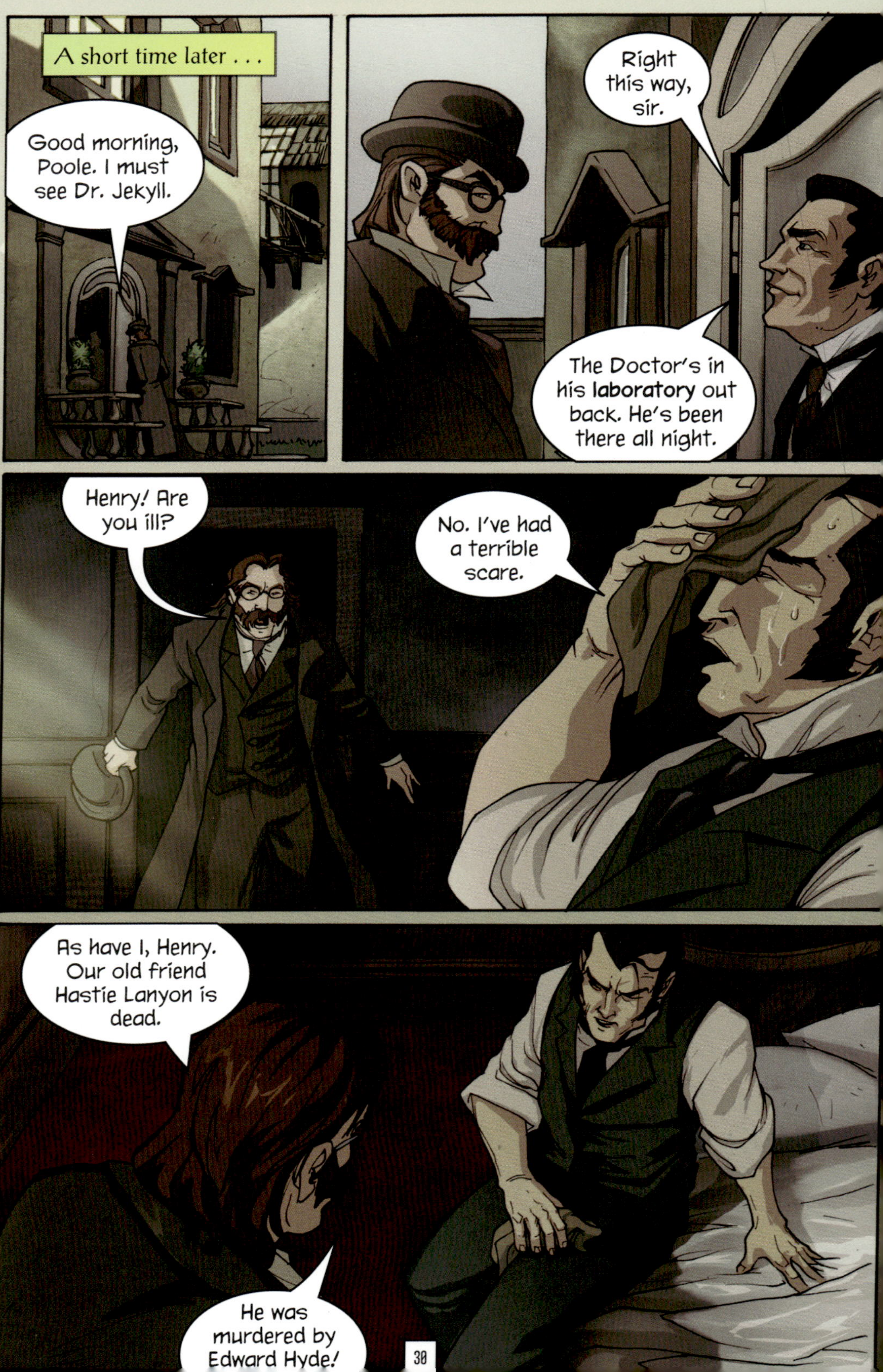
A short time later . . .
Good morning, Poole. I must see Dr. Jekyll.
Right this way, sir.
The Doctor's in his **laboratory** out back. He's been there all night.
Henry! Are you ill?
No. I've had a terrible scare.
As have I, Henry. Our old friend Hastie Lanyon is dead.
He was murdered by Edward Hyde!

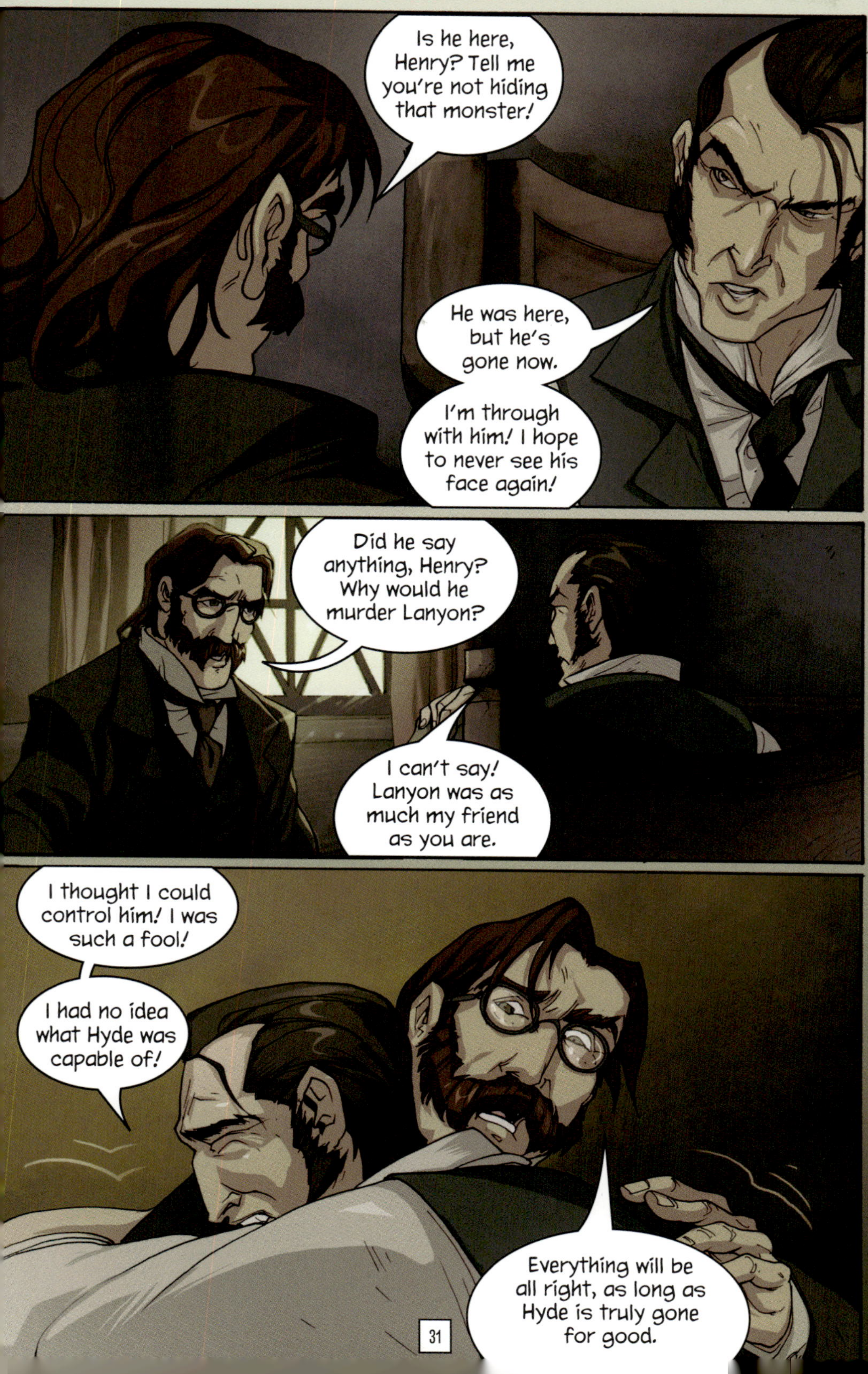

Is he here, Henry? Tell me you're not hiding that monster!
He was here, but he's gone now.
I'm through with him! I hope to never see his face again!
Did he say anything, Henry? Why would he murder Lanyon?
I can't say! Lanyon was as much my friend as you are.
I thought I could control him! I was such a fool!
I had no idea what Hyde was capable of!
Everything will be all right, as long as Hyde is truly gone for good.

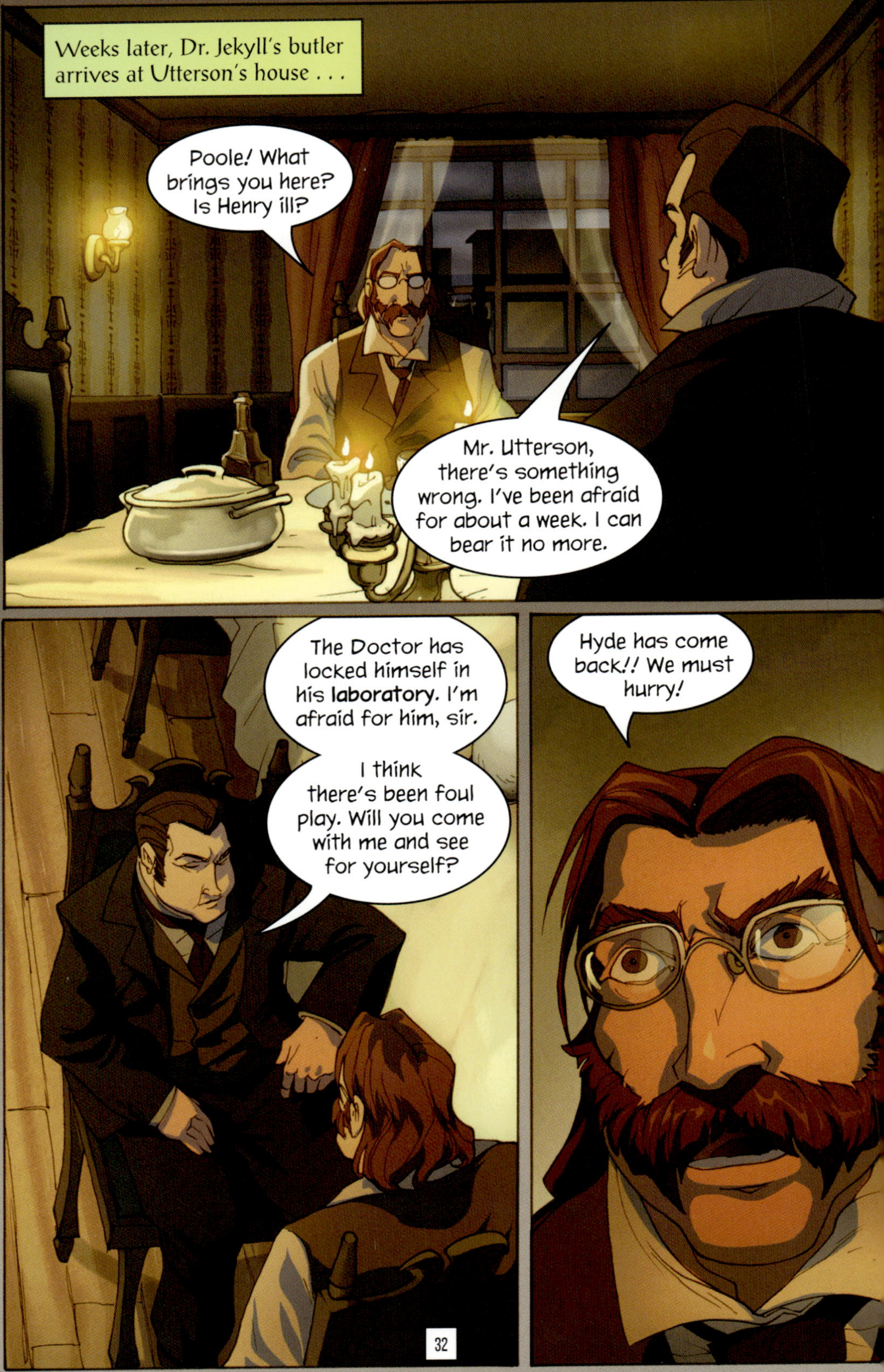
Weeks later, Dr. Jekyll's butler arrives at Utterson's house . . .
Poole! What brings you here? Is Henry ill?
Mr. Utterson, there's something wrong. I've been afraid for about a week. I can bear it no more.
The Doctor has locked himself in his **laboratory**. I'm afraid for him, sir.
I think there's been foul play. Will you come with me and see for yourself?
Hyde has come back!! We must hurry!

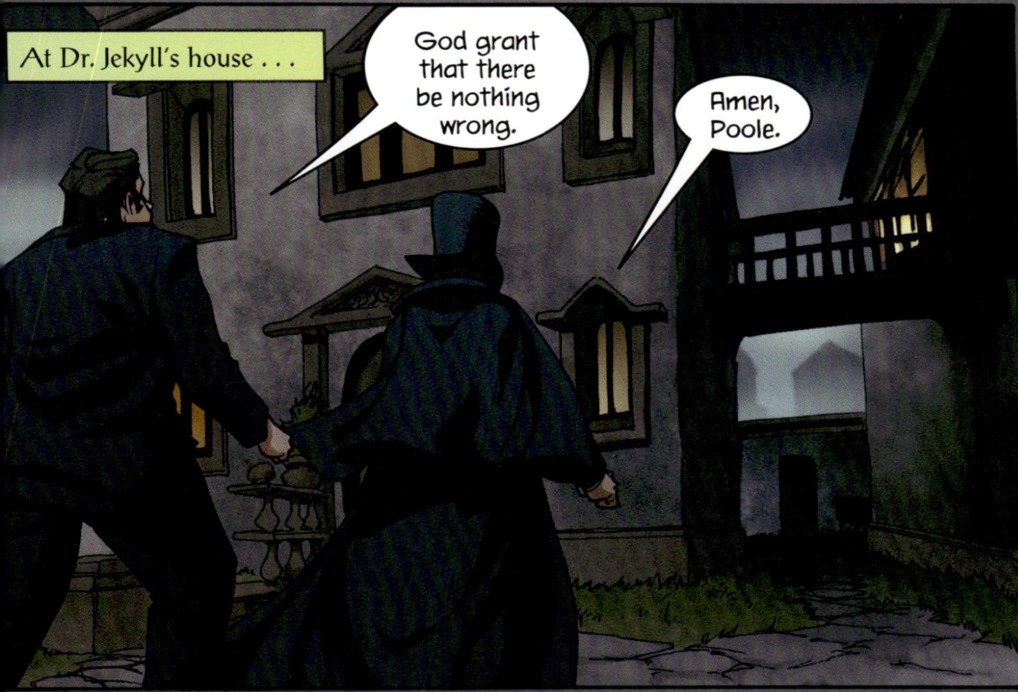
At Dr. Jekyll's house . . .
God grant that there be nothing wrong.
Amen, Poole.

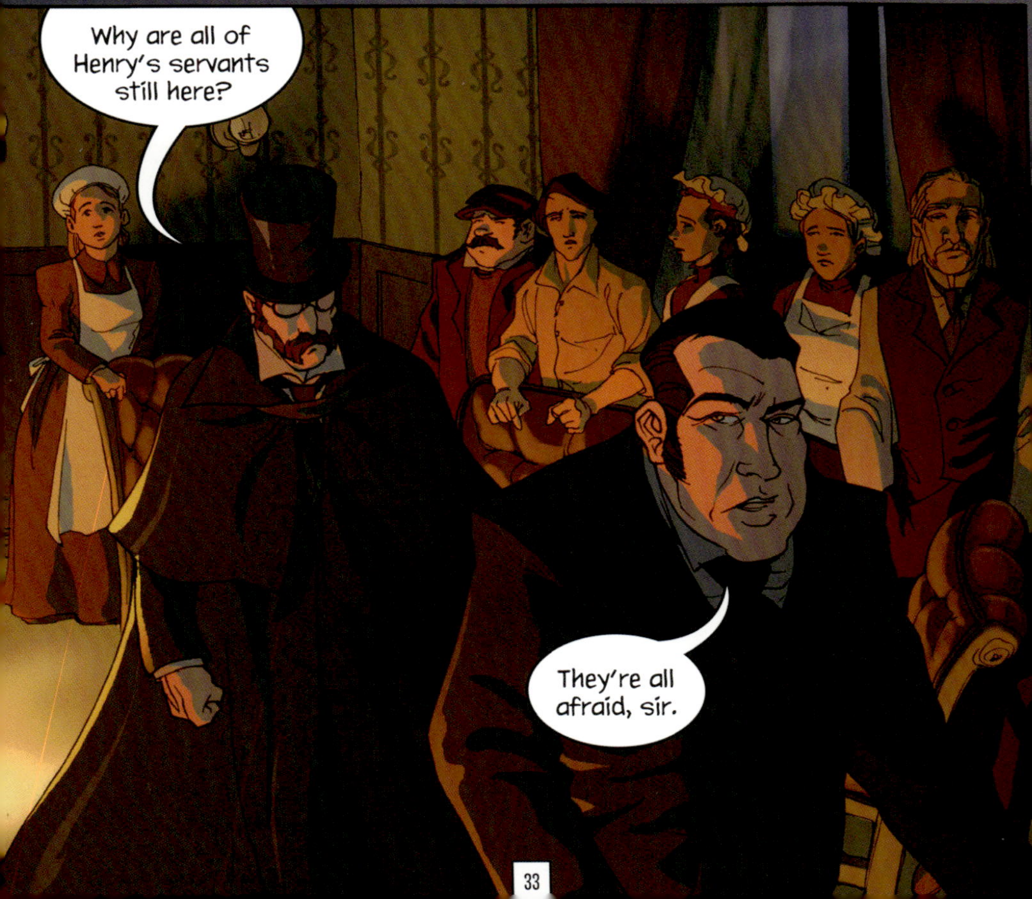
Why are all of Henry's servants still here?
They're all afraid, sir.

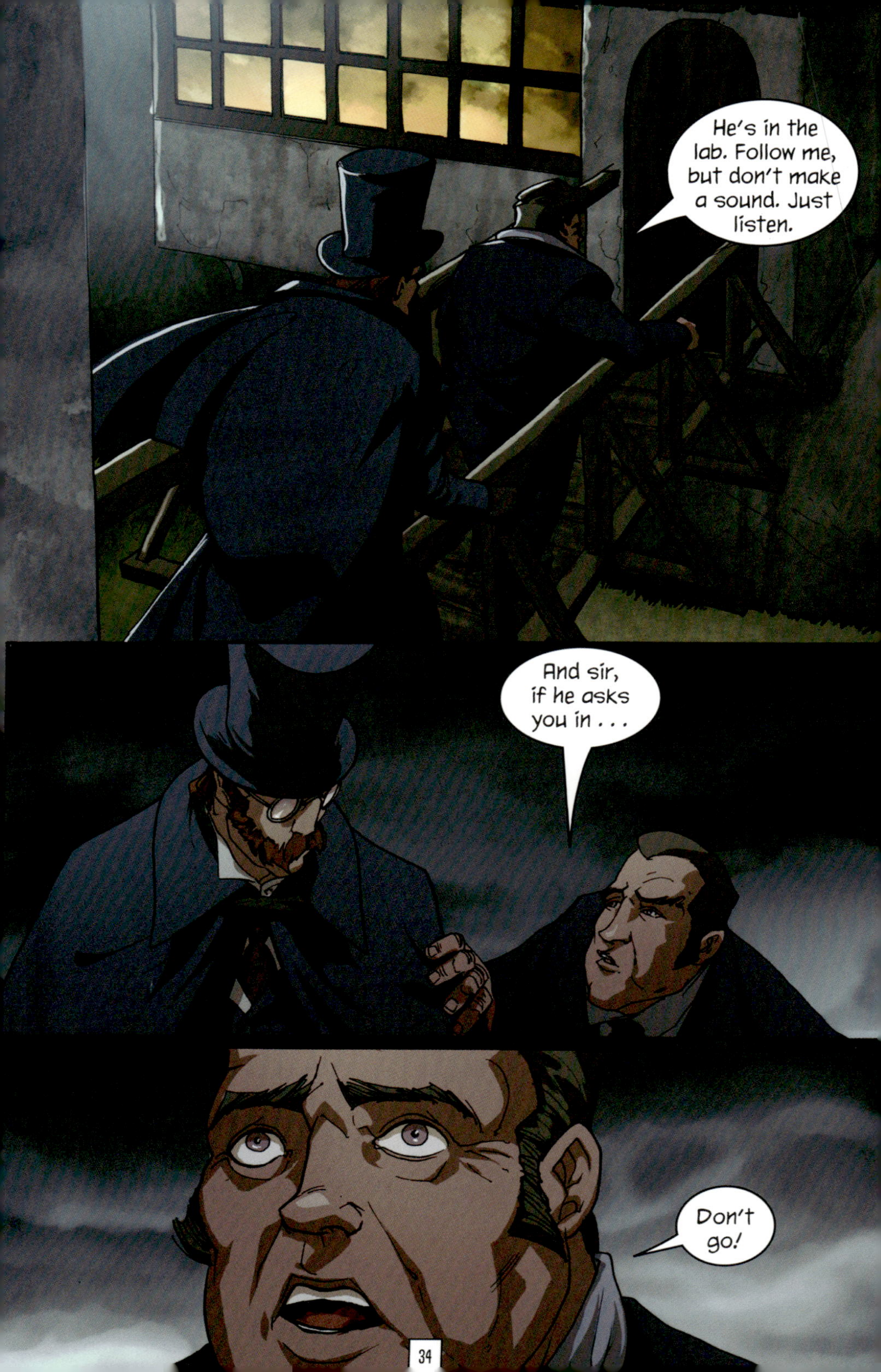
He's in the lab. Follow me, but don't make a sound. Just listen.
And sir, if he asks you in . . .
Don't go!

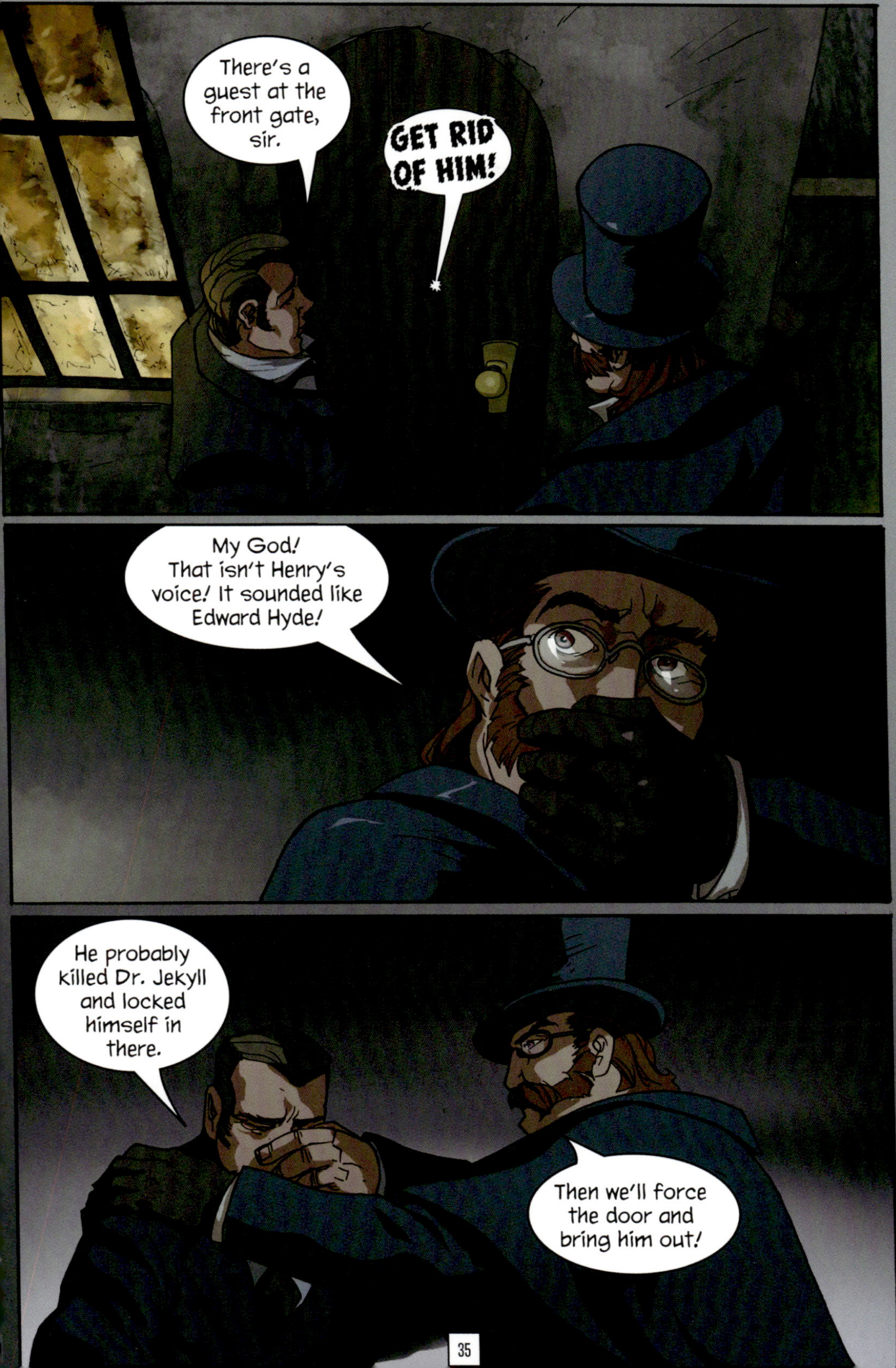
There's a guest at the front gate, sir.
GET RID OF HIM!
My God! That isn't Henry's voice! It sounded like Edward Hyde!
He probably killed Dr. Jekyll and locked himself in there.
Then we'll force the door and bring him out!

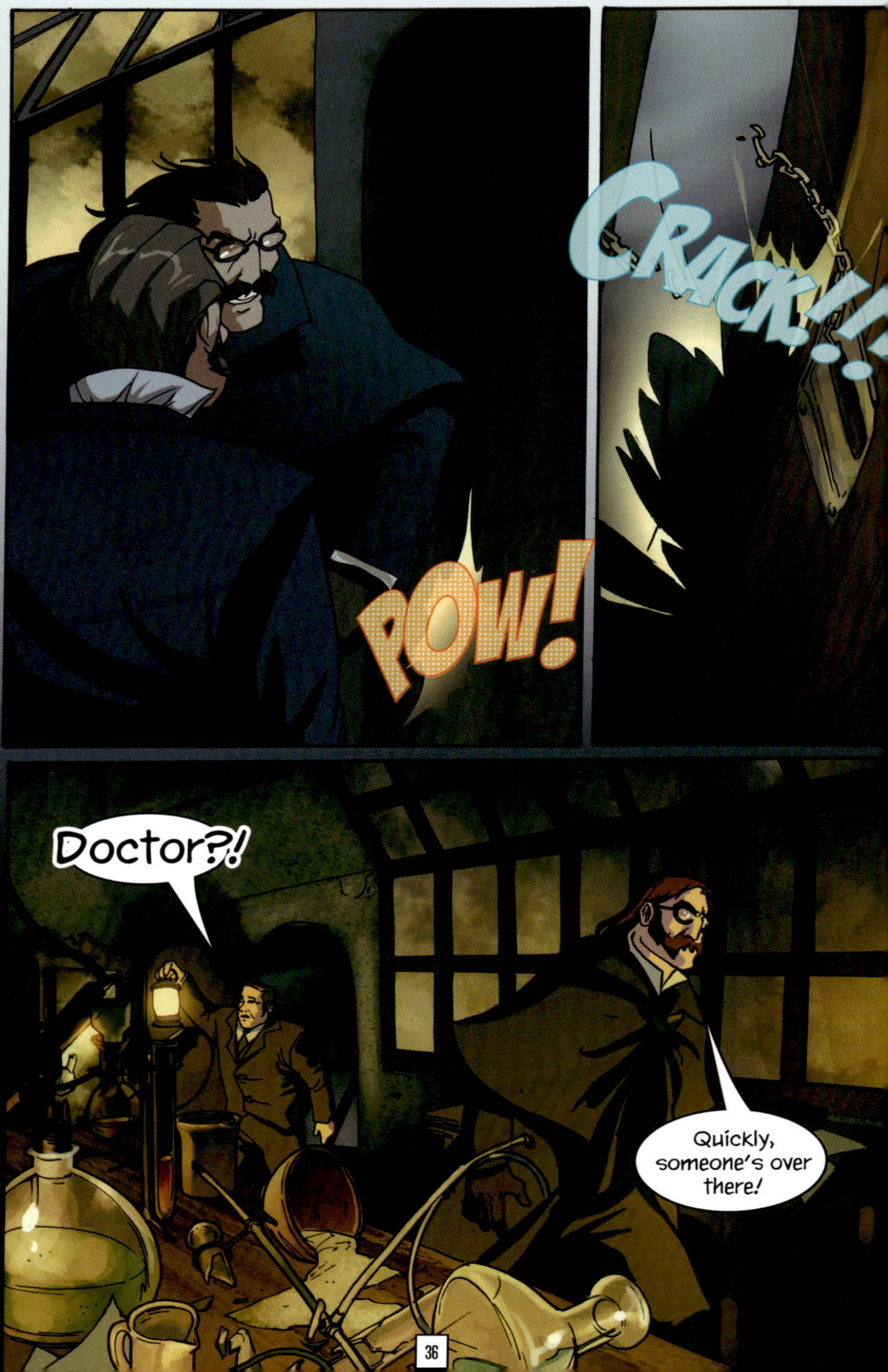
CRACK!!!
POW!
Doctor?!
Quickly, someone's over there!

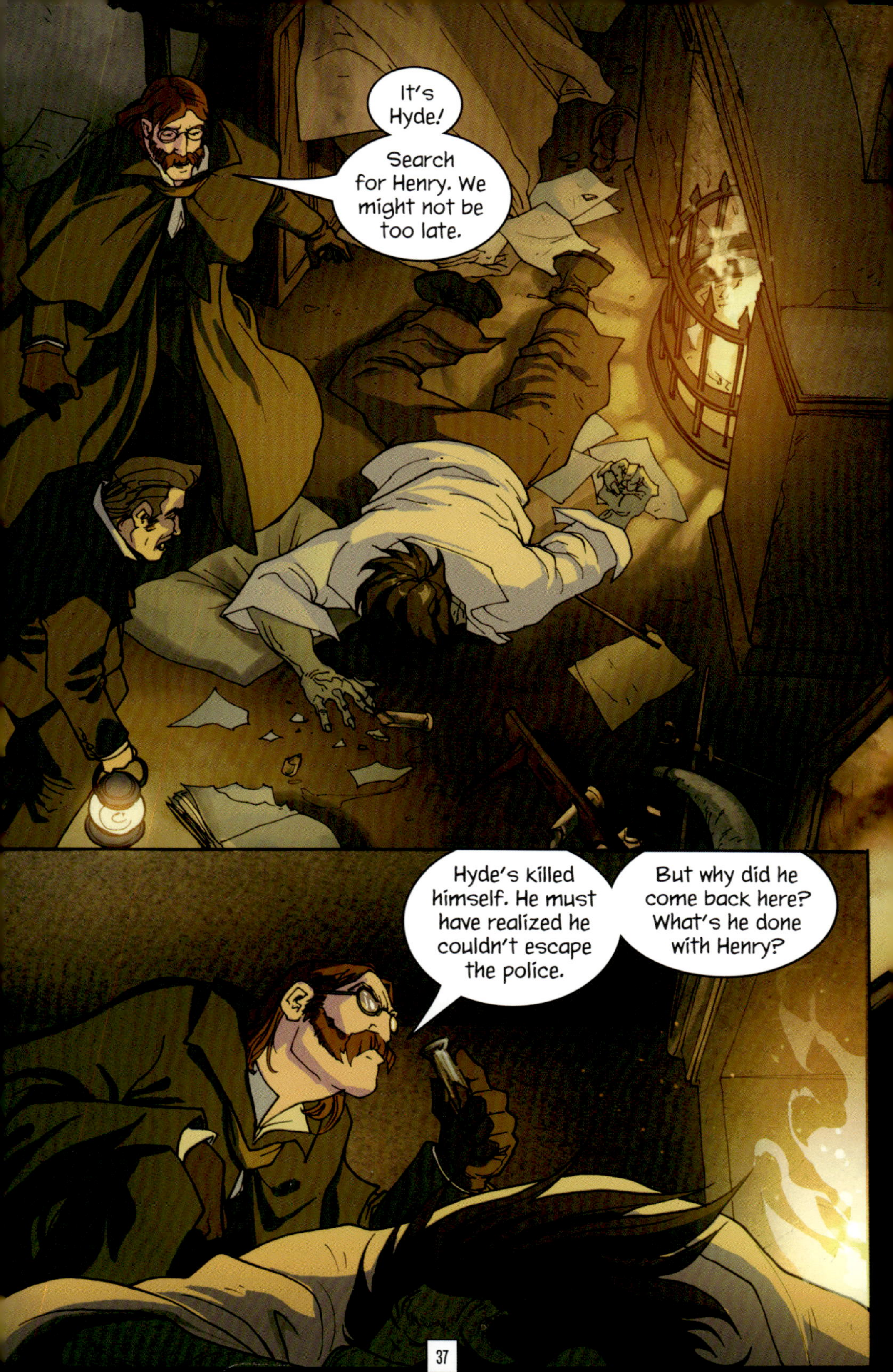
It's Hyde!
Search for Henry. We might not be too late.
Hyde's killed himself. He must have realized he couldn't escape the police.
But why did he come back here? What's he done with Henry?

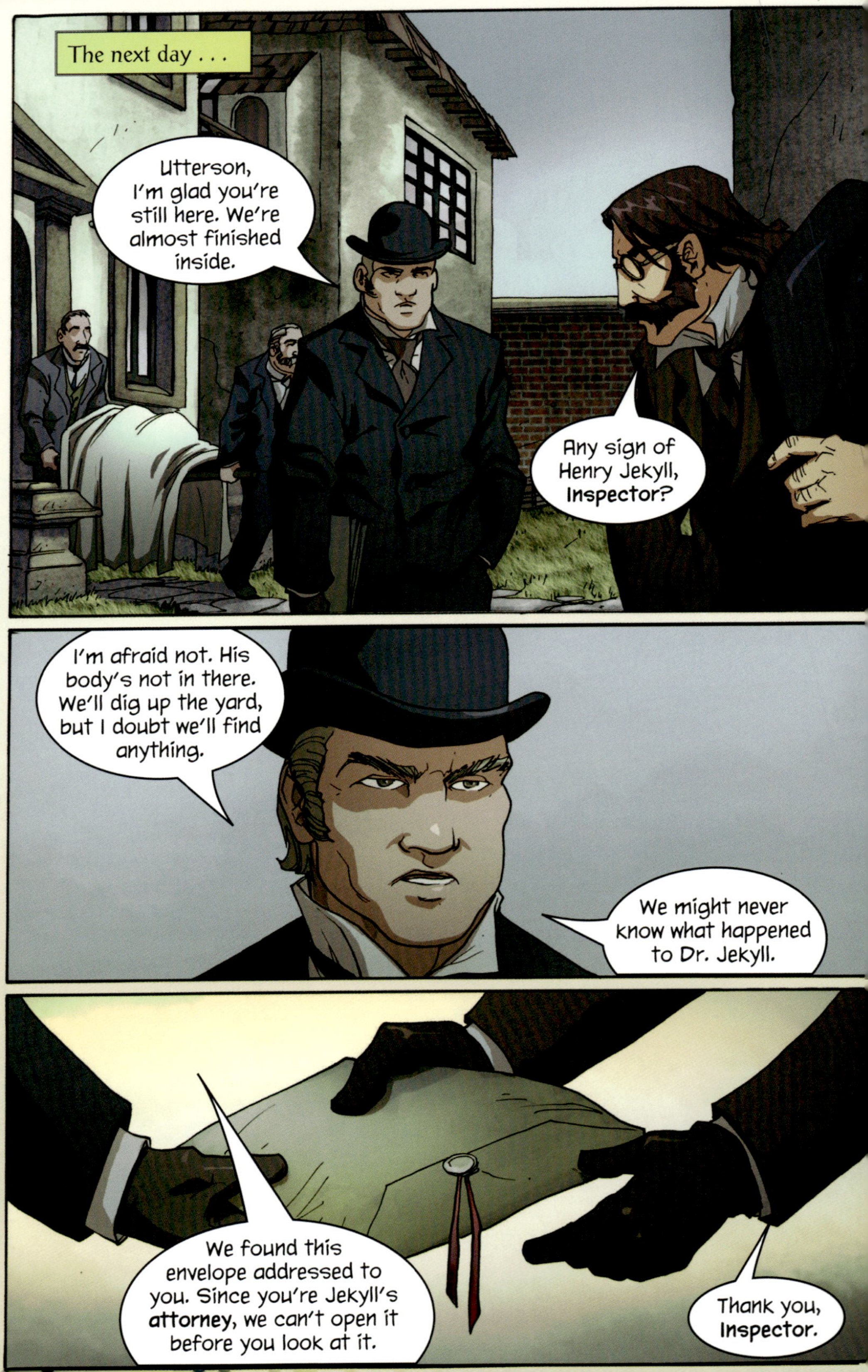
The next day . . .
Utterson, I'm glad you're still here. We're almost finished inside.
Any sign of Henry Jekyll, **Inspector**?
I'm afraid not. His body's not in there. We'll dig up the yard, but I doubt we'll find anything.
We might never know what happened to Dr. Jekyll.
We found this envelope addressed to you. Since you're Jekyll's **attorney**, we can't open it before you look at it.
Thank you, **Inspector**.

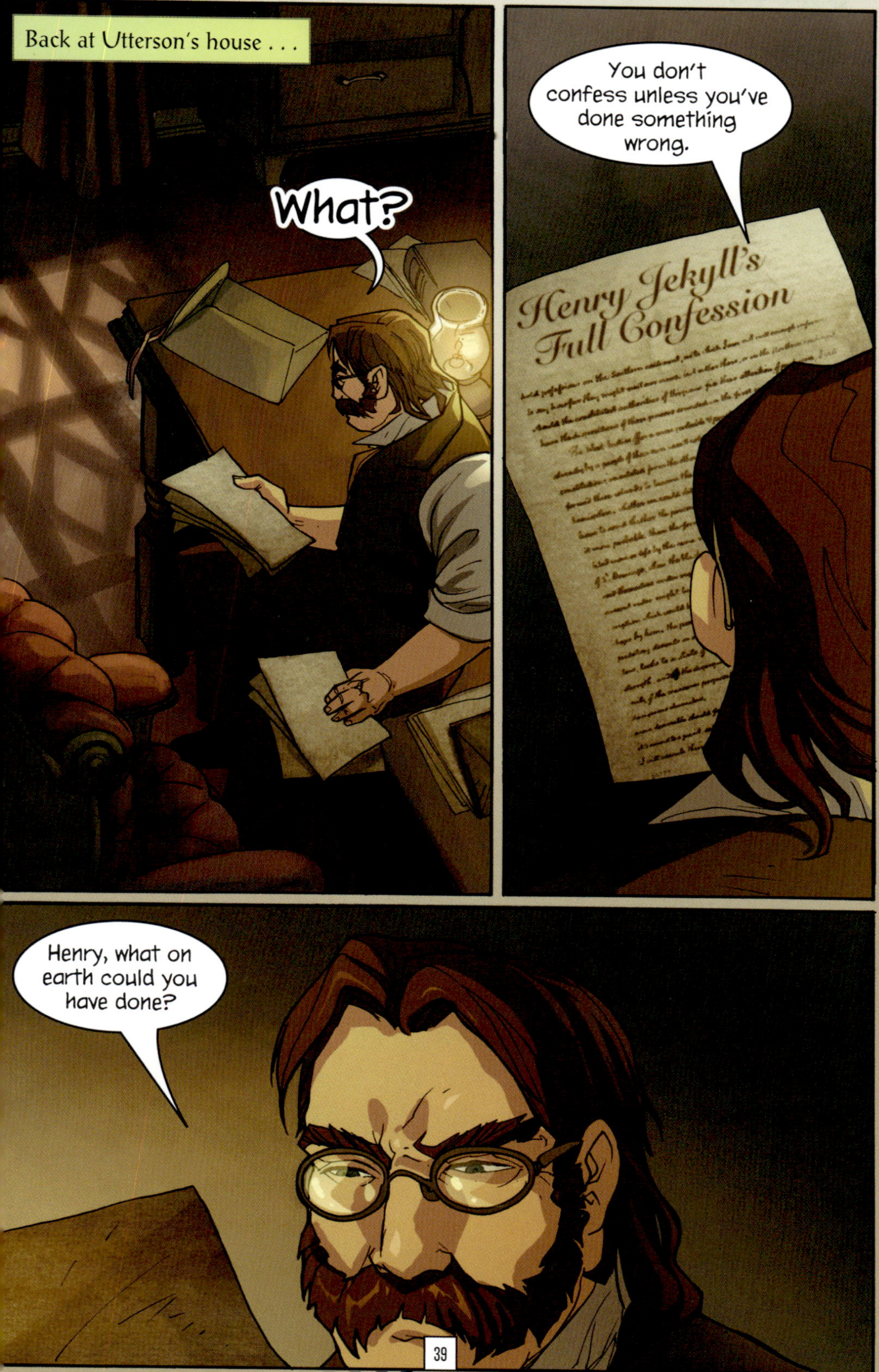
Back at Utterson's house . . .
What?
You don't confess unless you've done something wrong.
Henry Jekyll's Full Confession
Henry, what on earth could you have done?

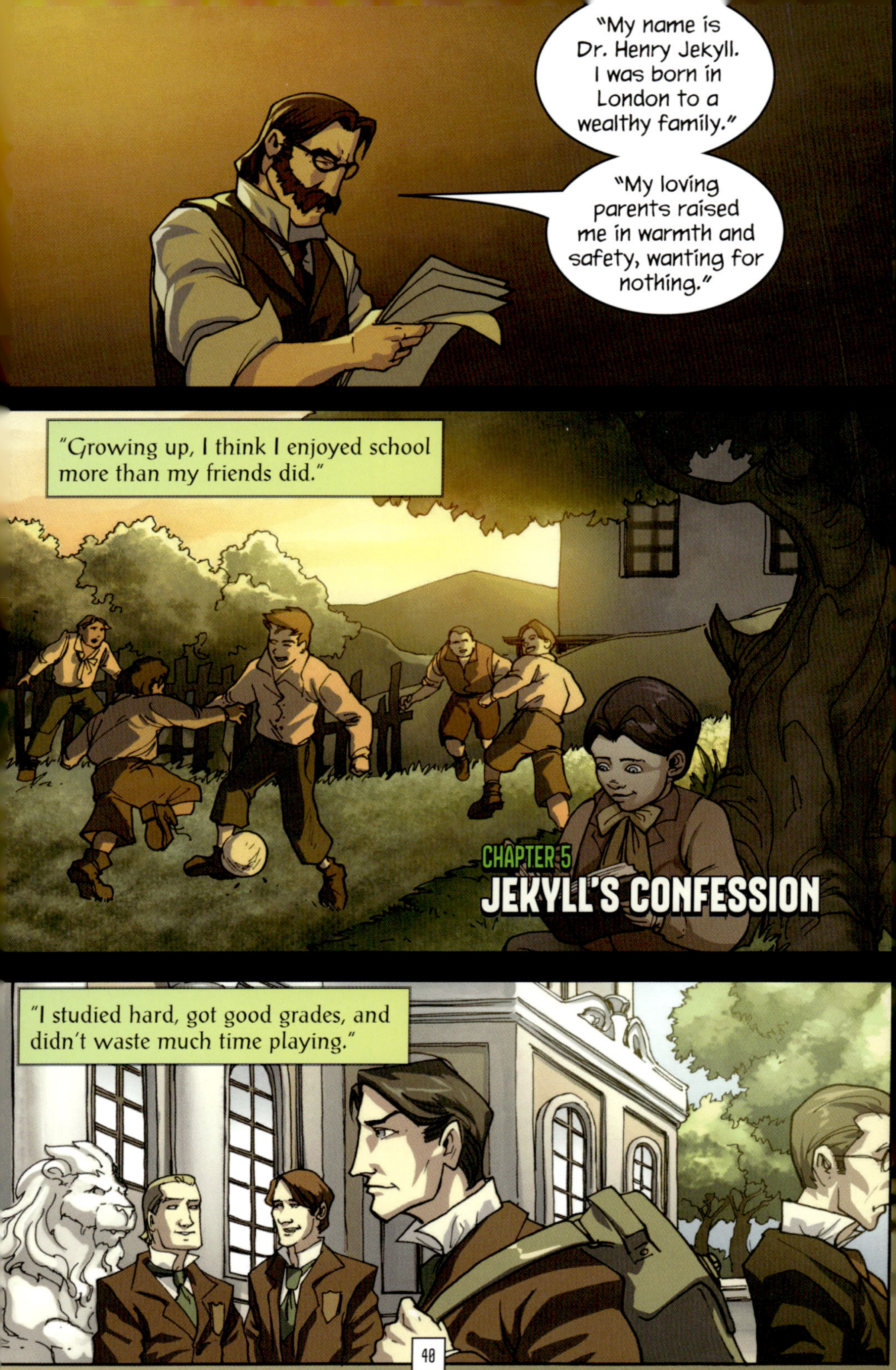
"My name is Dr. Henry Jekyll. I was born in London to a wealthy family."
"My loving parents raised me in warmth and safety, wanting for nothing."
"Growing up, I think I enjoyed school more than my friends did."
CHAPTER 5
JEKYLL'S CONFESSION
"I studied hard, got good grades, and didn't waste much time playing."

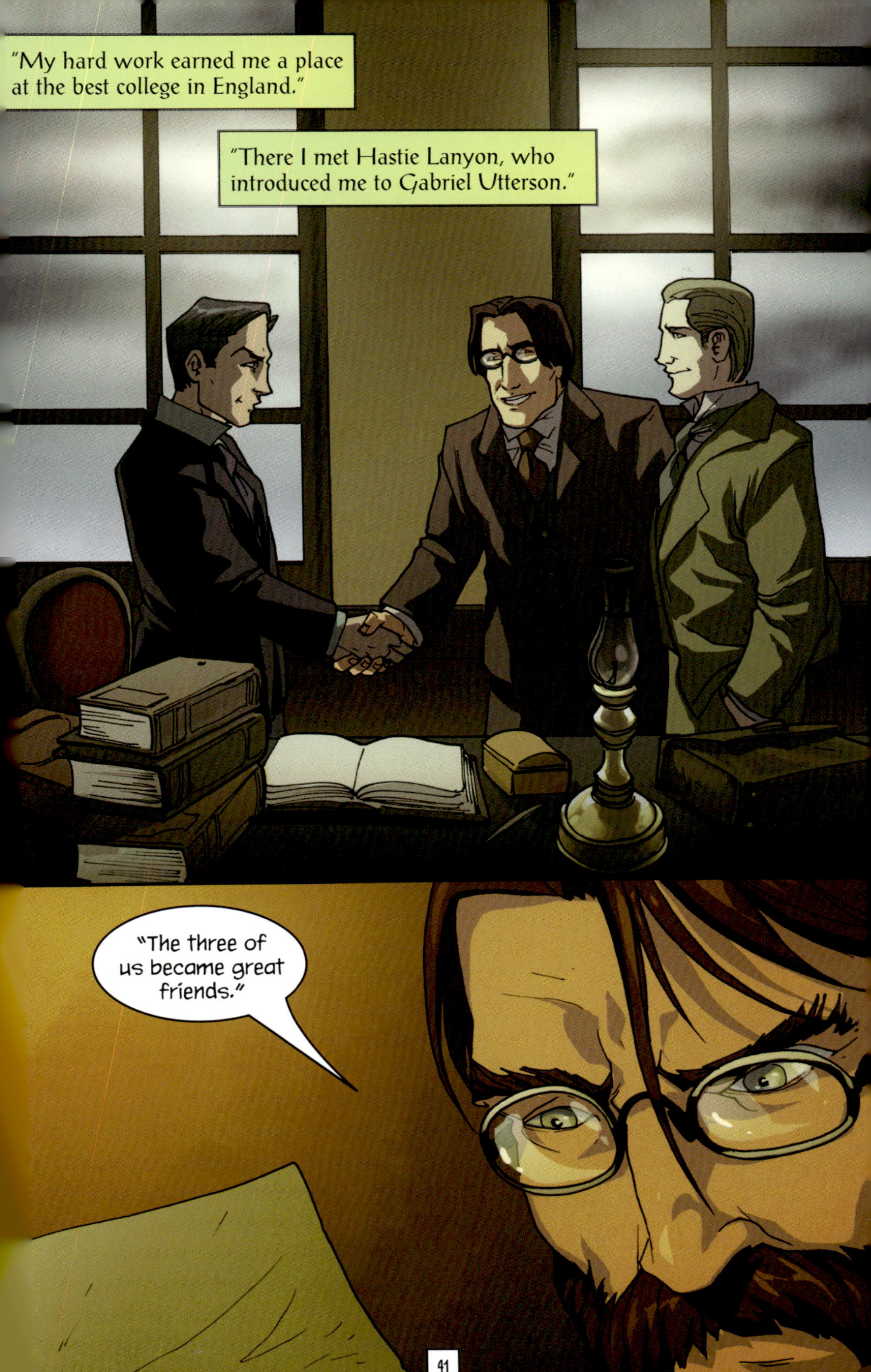
"My hard work earned me a place at the best college in England."
"There I met Hastie Lanyon, who introduced me to Gabriel Utterson."
"The three of us became great friends."

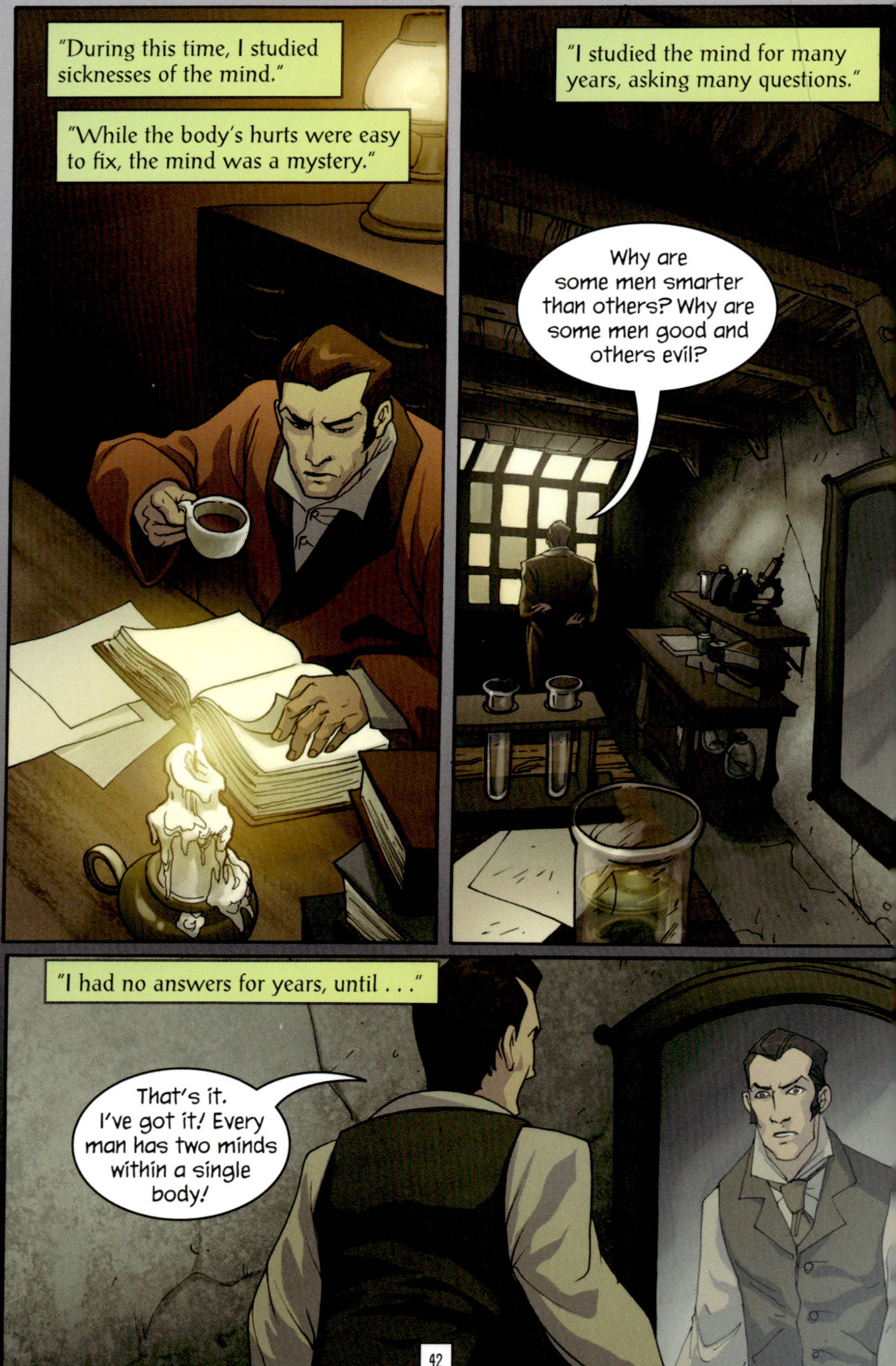

"During this time, I studied sicknesses of the mind."
"While the body's hurts were easy to fix, the mind was a mystery."
"I studied the mind for many years, asking many questions."
Why are some men smarter than others? Why are some men good and others evil?
"I had no answers for years, until . . ."
That's it. I've got it! Every man has two minds within a single body!

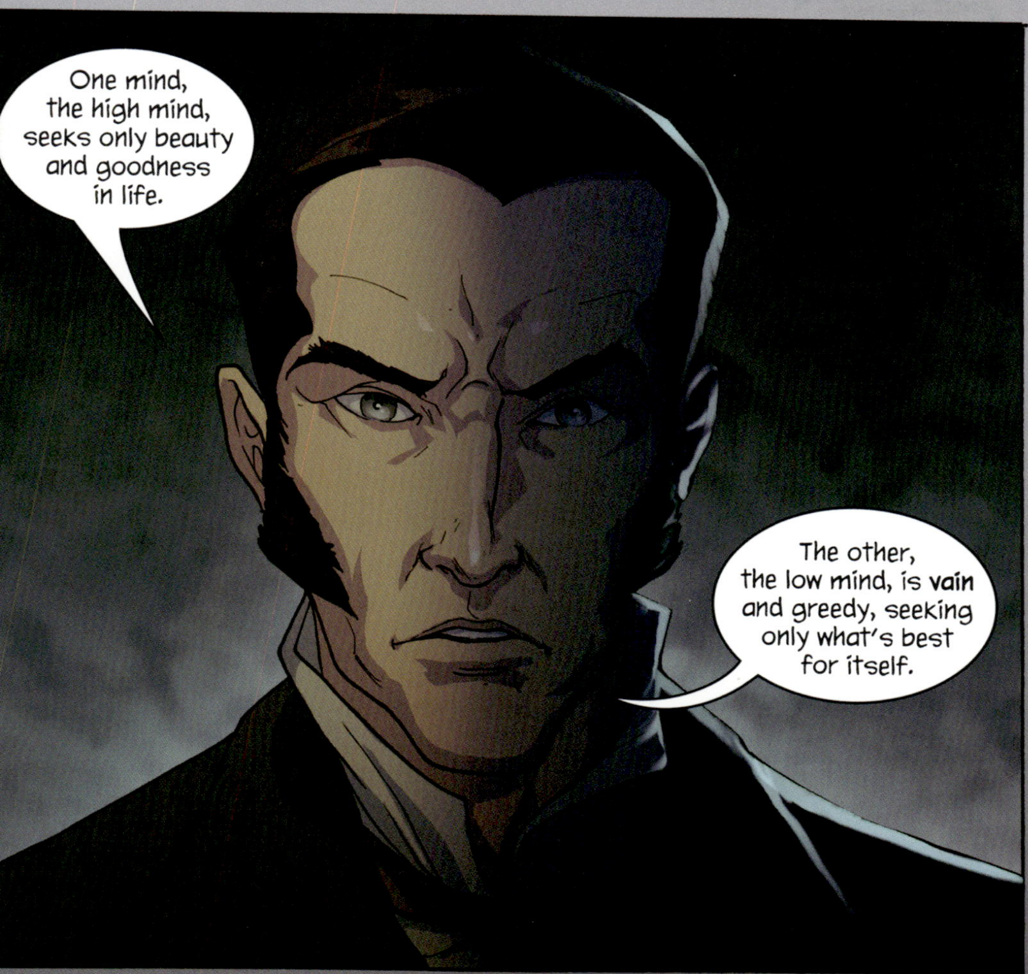
One mind, the high mind, seeks only beauty and goodness in life.
The other, the low mind, is **vain** and greedy, seeking only what's best for itself.

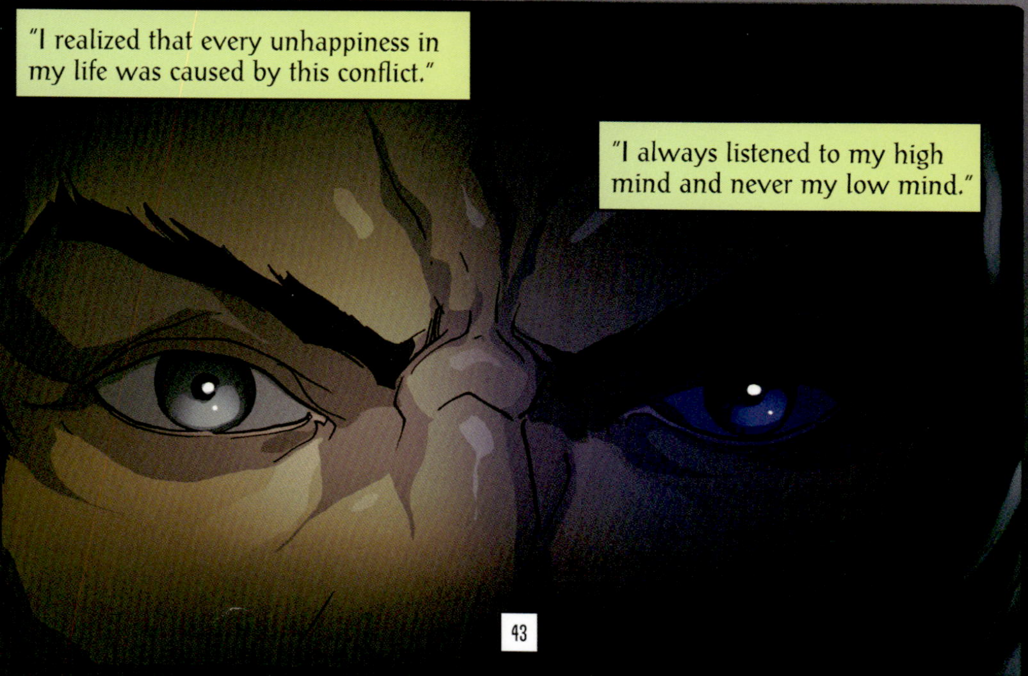
"I realized that every unhappiness in my life was caused by this conflict."
"I always listened to my high mind and never my low mind."

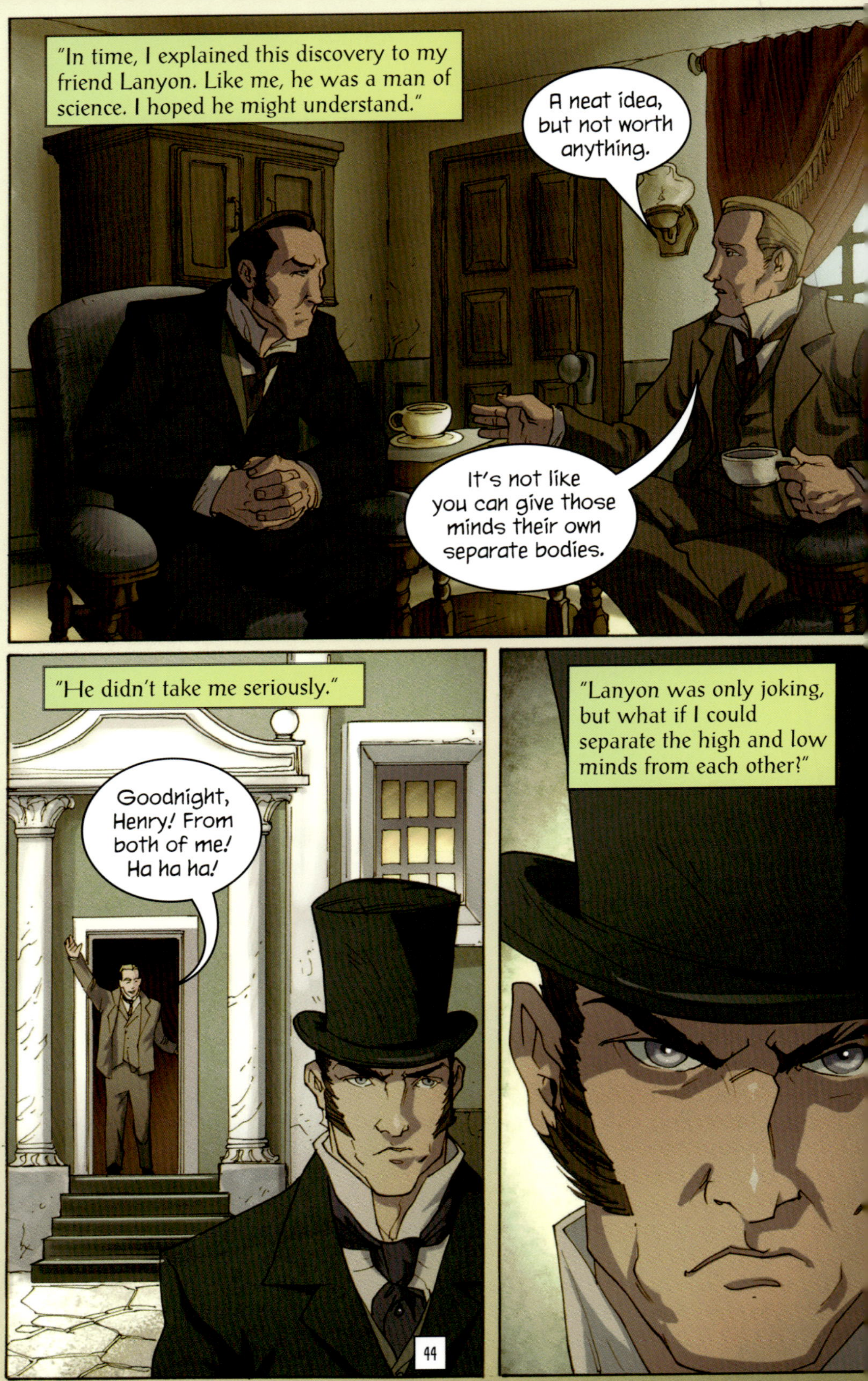
"In time, I explained this discovery to my friend Lanyon. Like me, he was a man of science. I hoped he might understand."
A neat idea, but not worth anything.
It's not like you can give those minds their own separate bodies.
"He didn't take me seriously."
Goodnight, Henry! From both of me! Ha ha ha!
"Lanyon was only joking, but what if I could separate the high and low minds from each other?"

"I set out at once to work on this scientific challenge."

"The key was a certain rare salt I'd found from halfway around the world."

"I can't be more specific about the **formula** I created. I won't. I can promise you, however, that it worked."

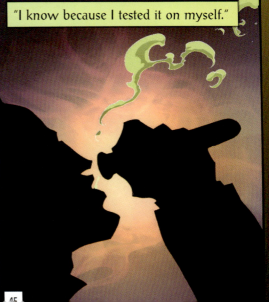

"I know because I tested it on myself."

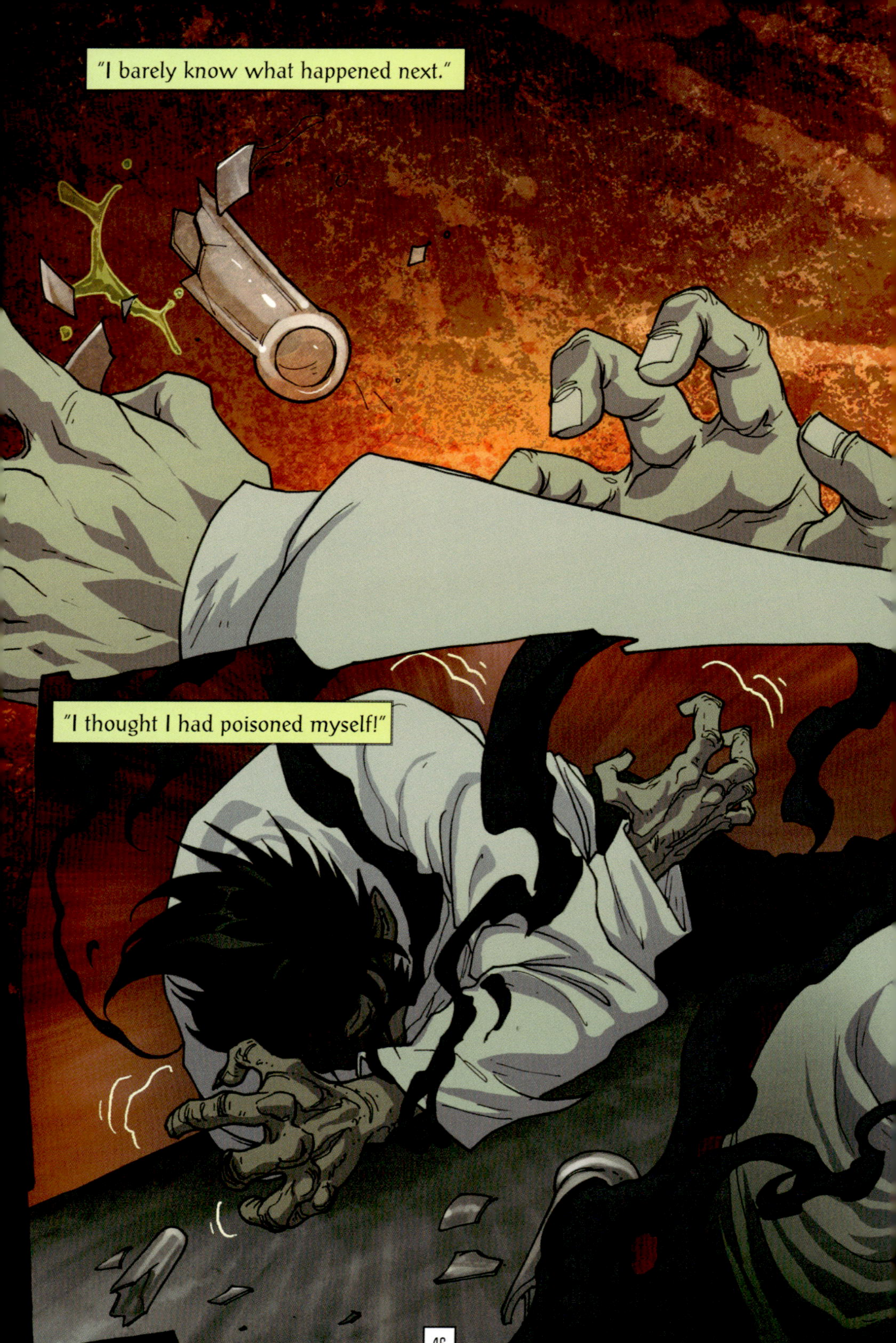
"I barely know what happened next."
"I thought I had poisoned myself!"

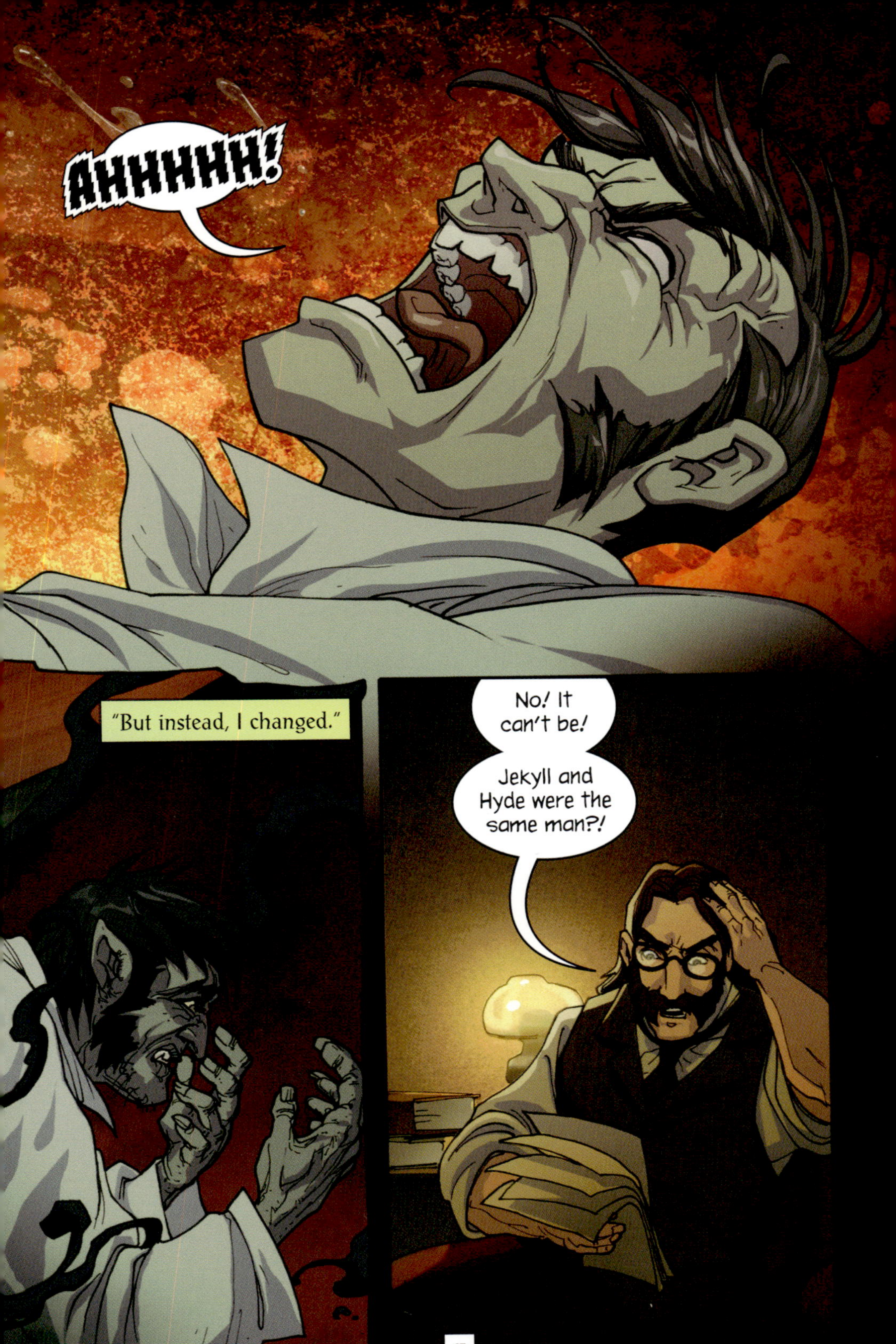
AHHHHH!
"But instead, I changed."
No! It can't be!
Jekyll and Hyde were the same man?!

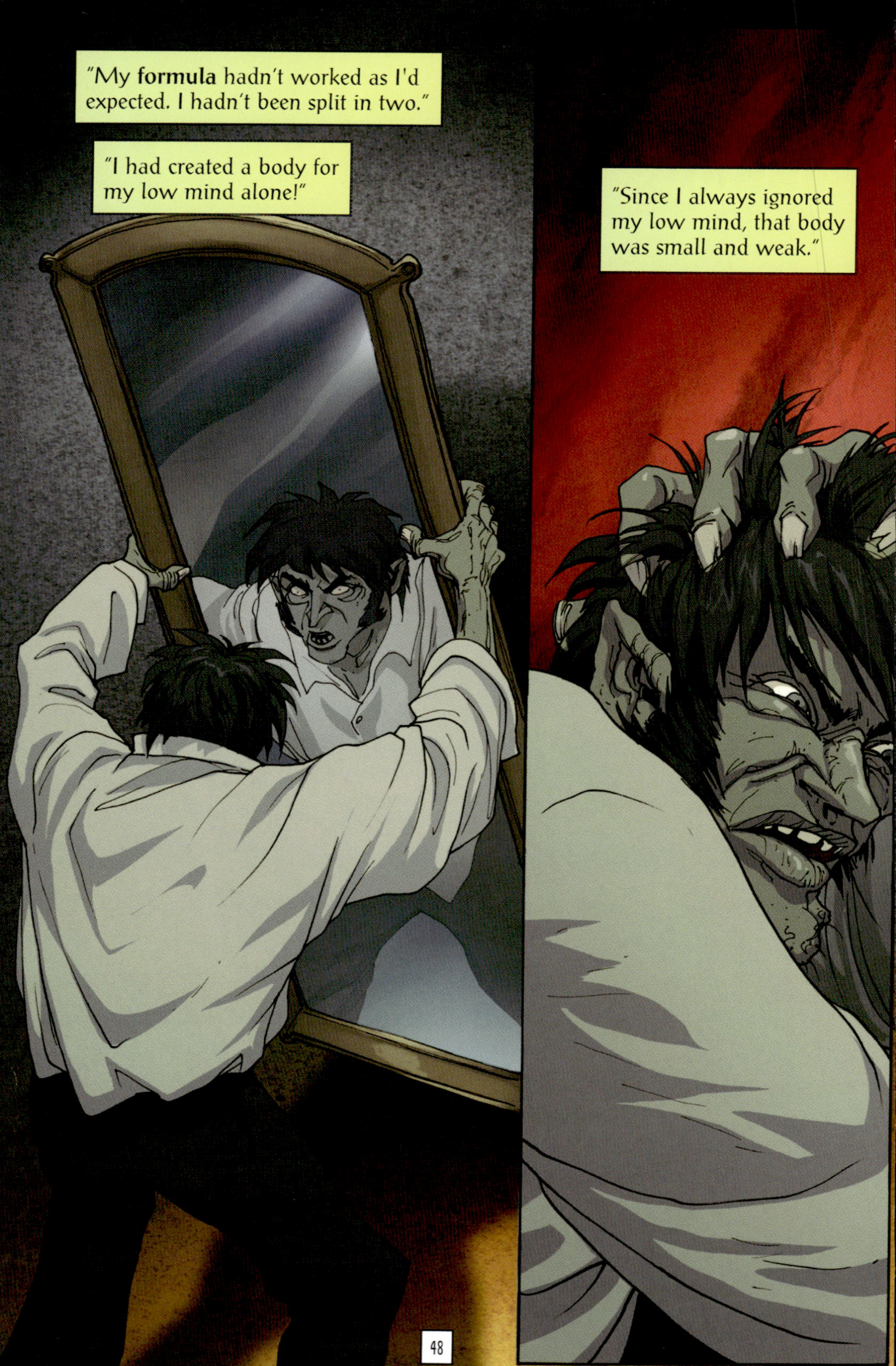
"My formula hadn't worked as I'd expected. I hadn't been split in two."
"I had created a body for my low mind alone!"
"Since I always ignored my low mind, that body was small and weak."

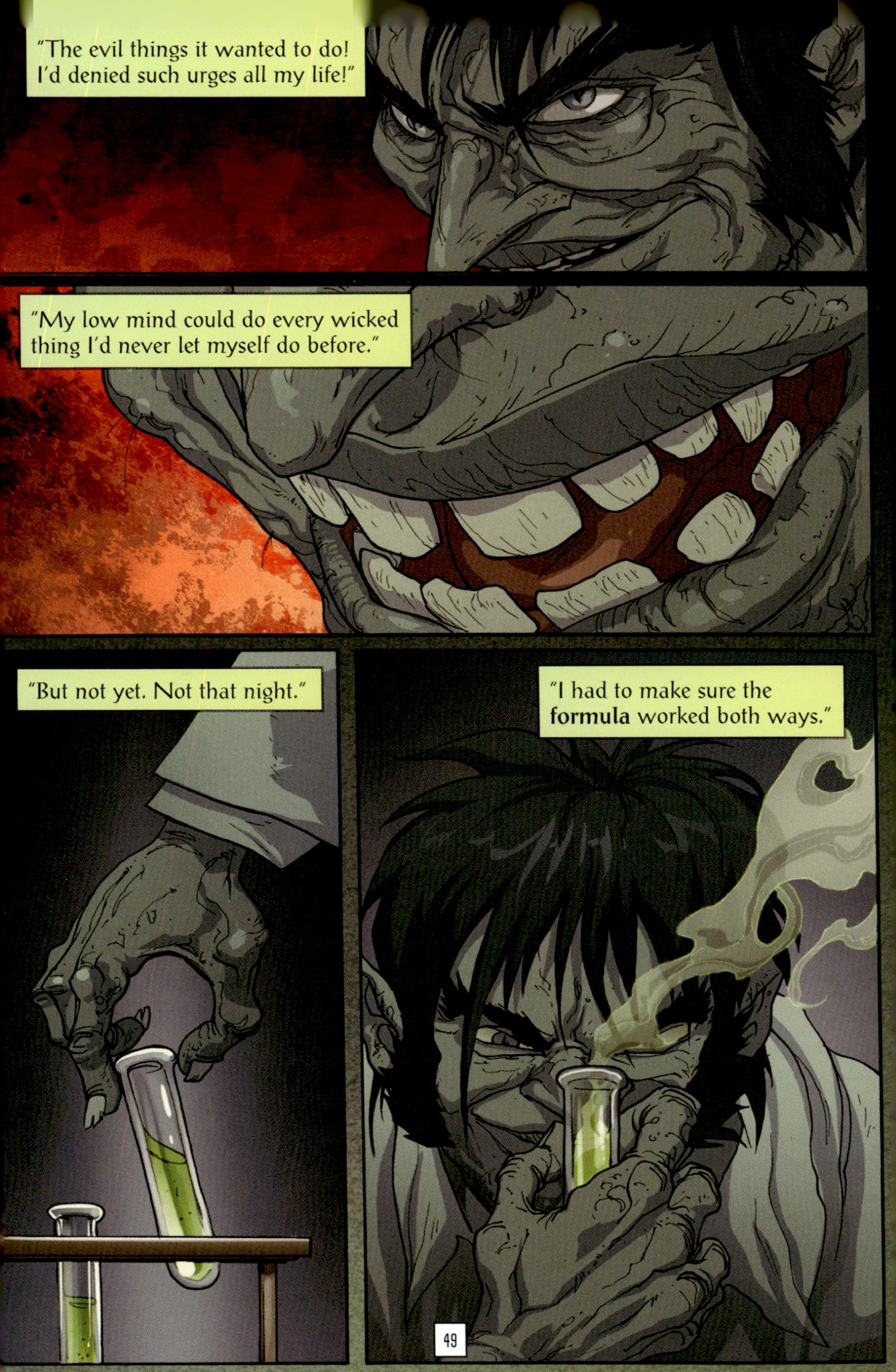
"The evil things it wanted to do! I'd denied such urges all my life!"
"My low mind could do every wicked thing I'd never let myself do before."
"But not yet. Not that night."
"I had to make sure the **formula** worked both ways."

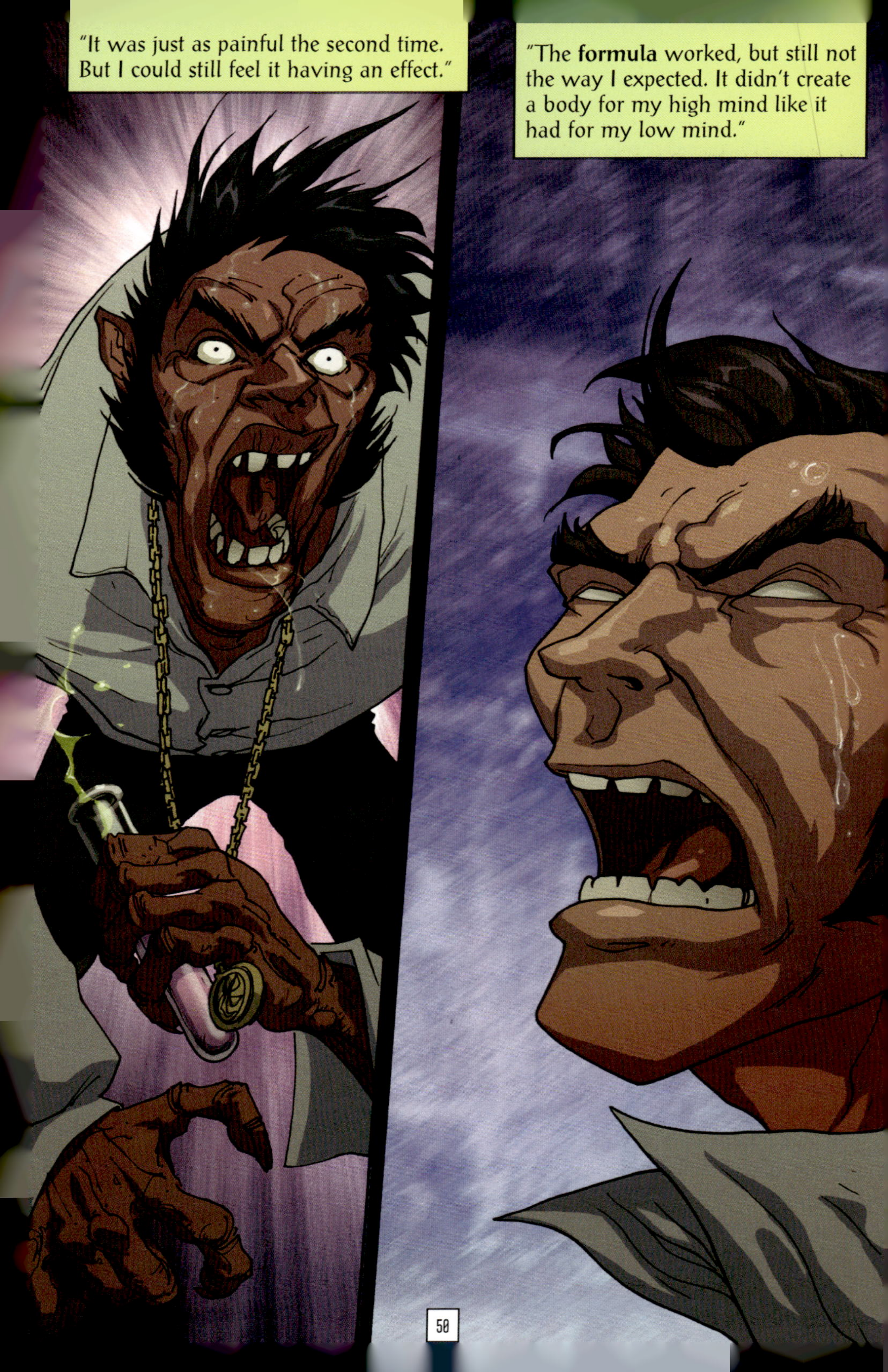
"It was just as painful the second time. But I could still feel it having an effect."
"The **formula** worked, but still not the way I expected. It didn't create a body for my high mind like it had for my low mind."

"I simply became myself again."

"But that was good enough for me."

"Soon, I began using my **formula** every day. I even changed my name to Edward Hyde because I acted like a completely separate person."

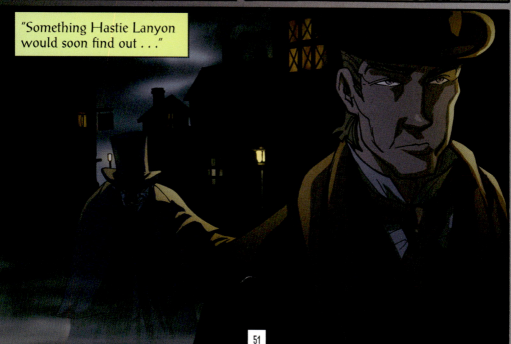

"Something Hastie Lanyon would soon find out . . ."

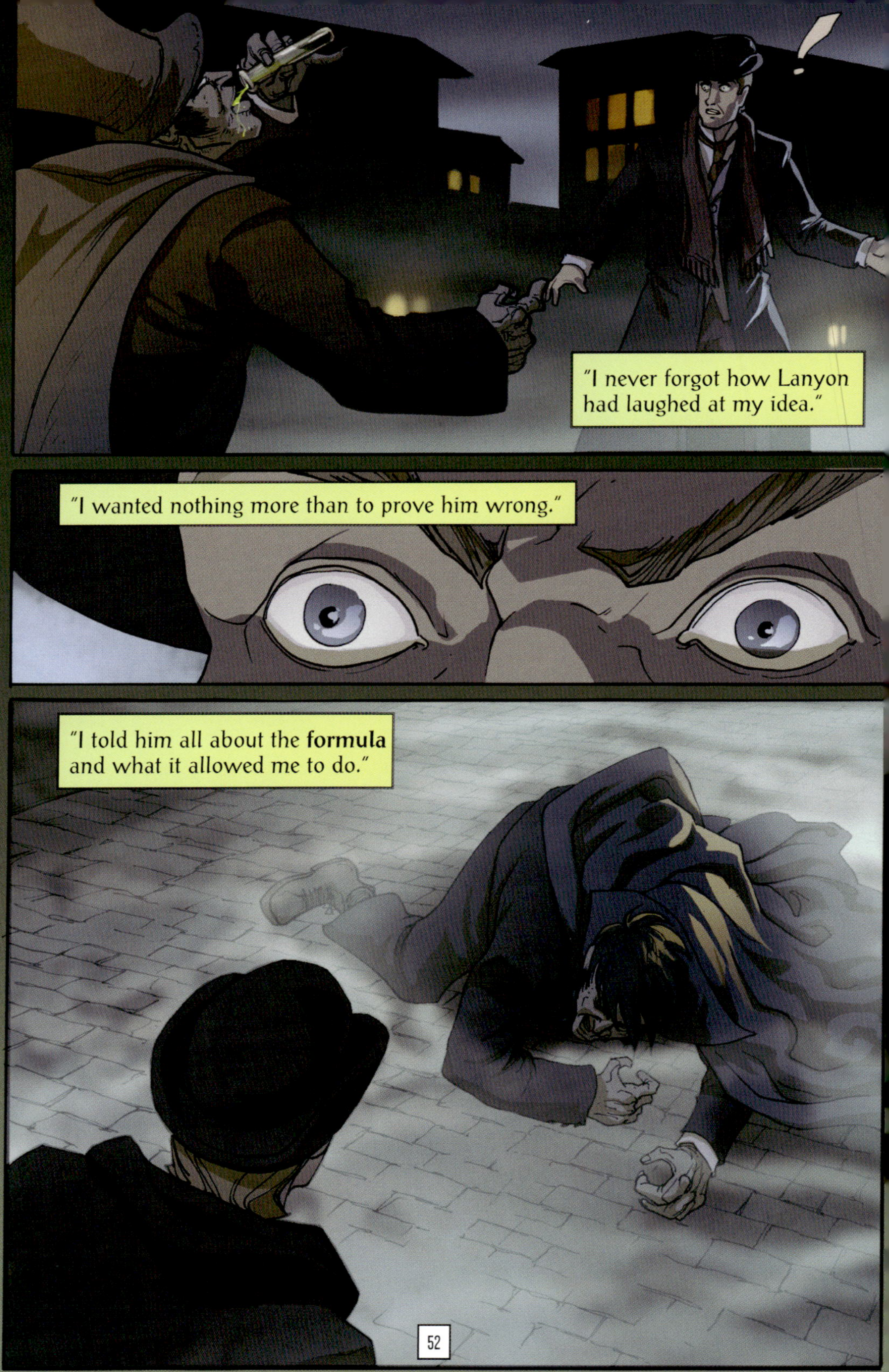
"I never forgot how Lanyon had laughed at my idea."
"I wanted nothing more than to prove him wrong."
"I told him all about the **formula** and what it allowed me to do."

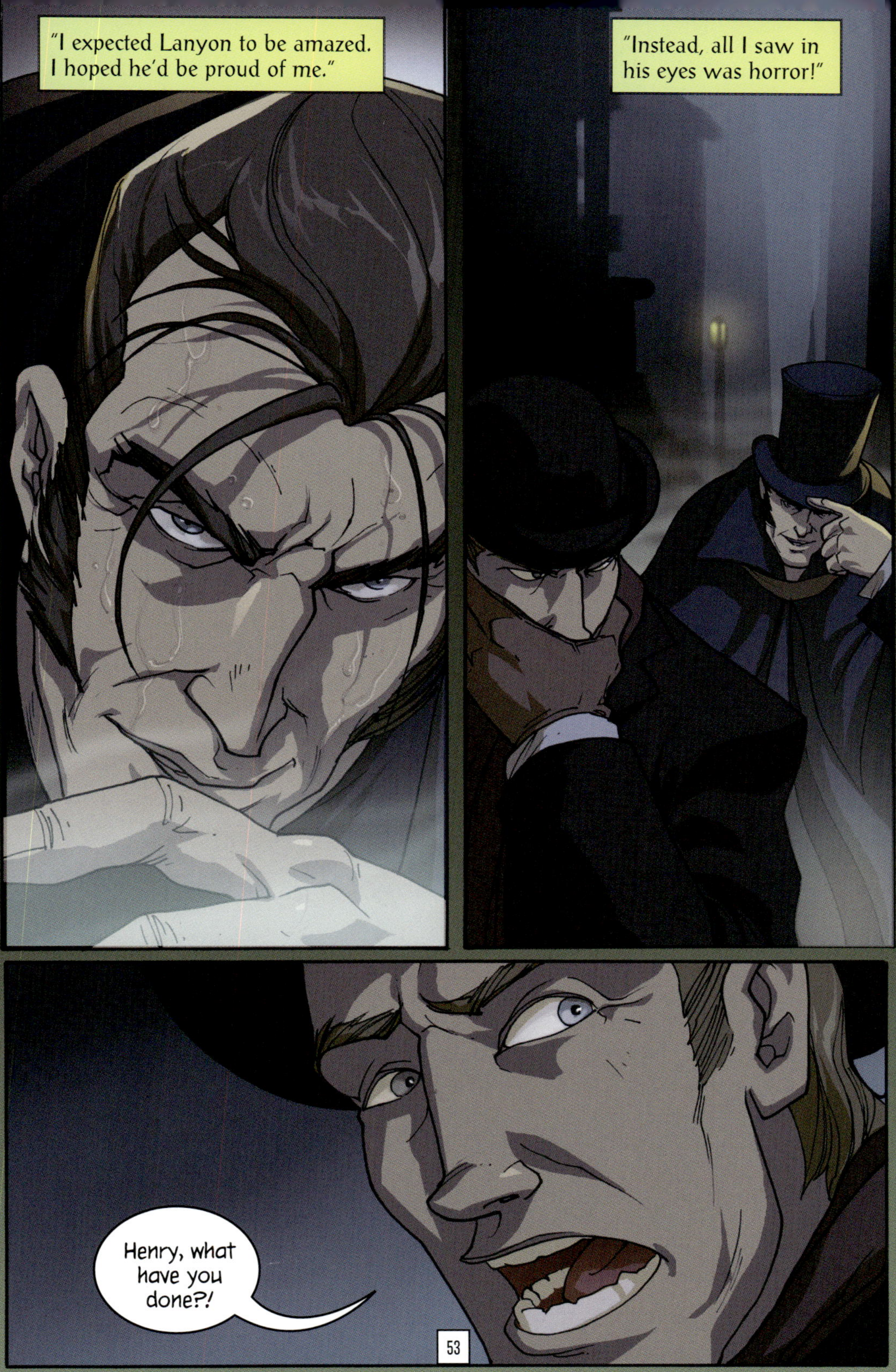
"I expected Lanyon to be amazed. I hoped he'd be proud of me."
"Instead, all I saw in his eyes was horror!"
Henry, what have you done?!

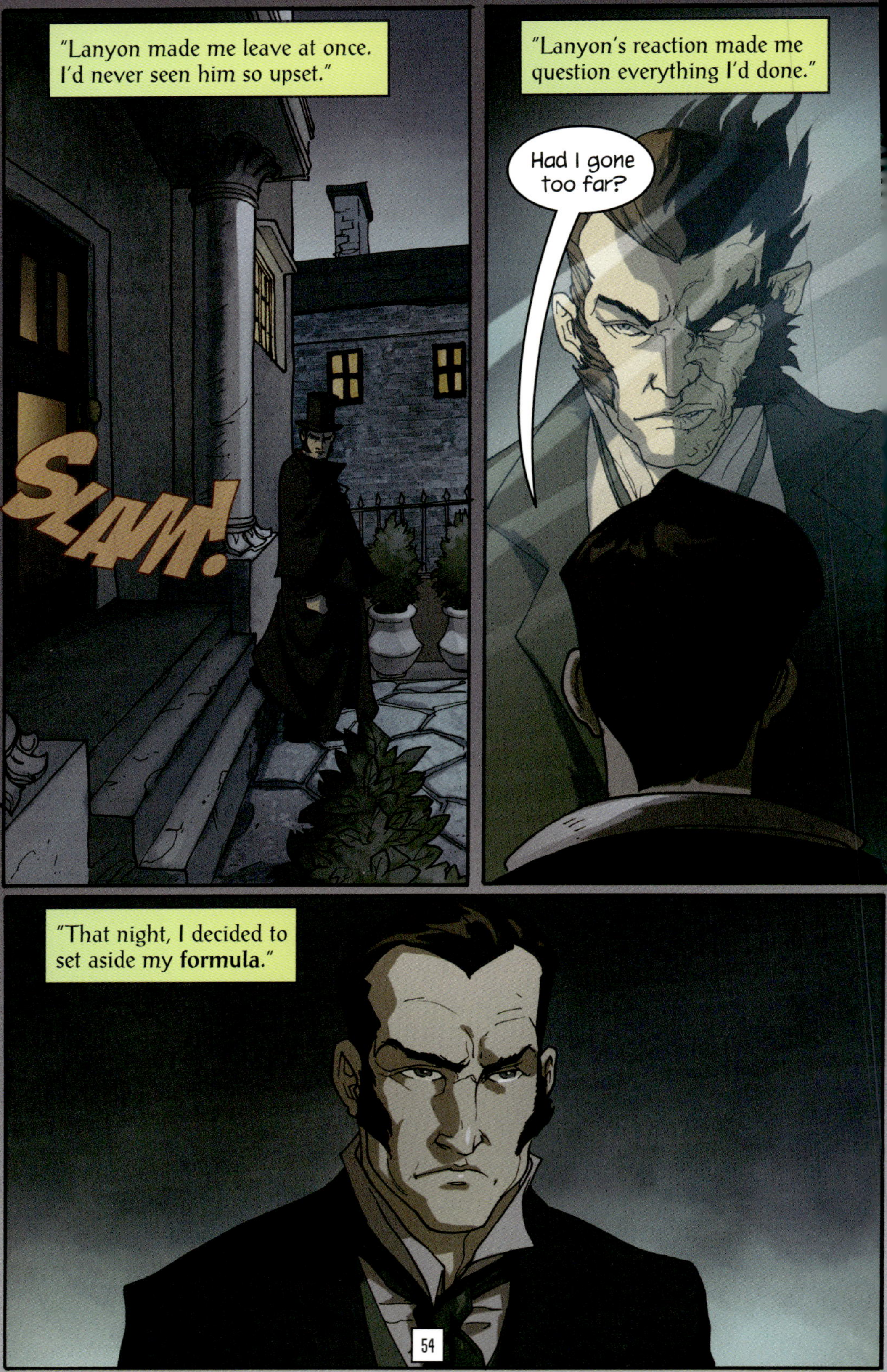
"Lanyon made me leave at once. I'd never seen him so upset."
SLAM!
"Lanyon's reaction made me question everything I'd done."
Had I gone too far?
"That night, I decided to set aside my **formula**."

"I woke the next day. To my relief, my low mind was blessedly quiet."

"But then . . ."

SSSSSSSSS

What on earth?

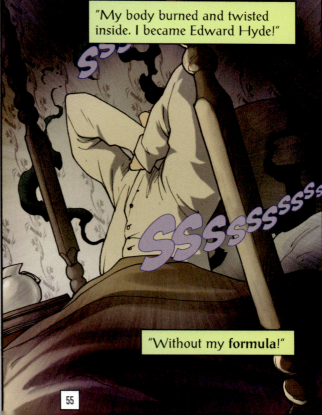

"My body burned and twisted inside. I became Edward Hyde!"

SSSSSSSSSS

"Without my **formula!**"

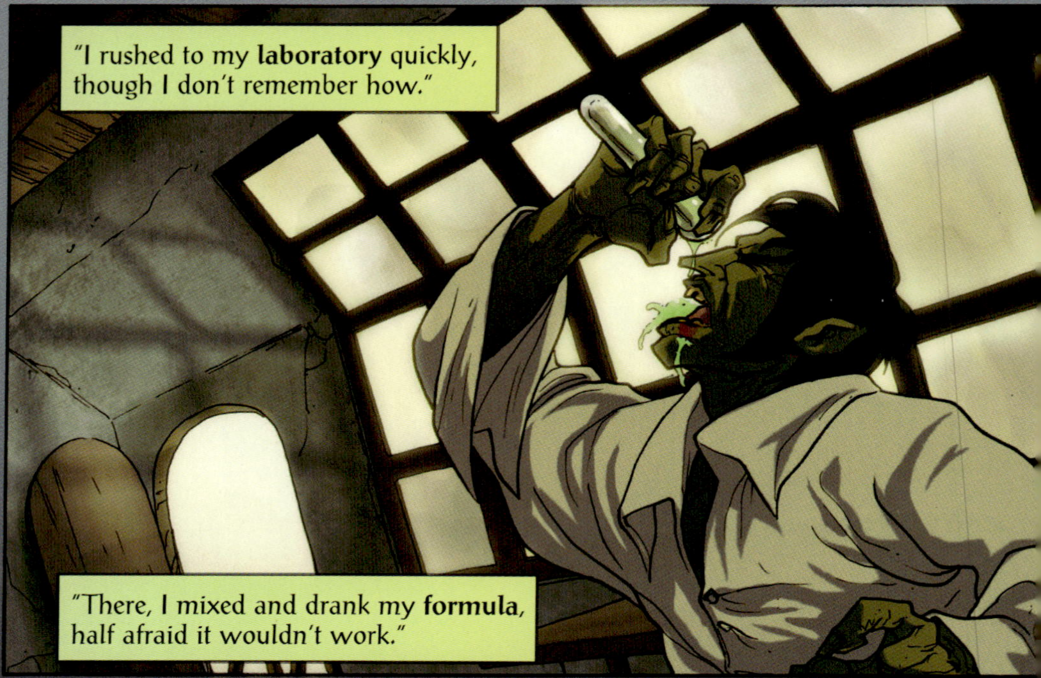
"I rushed to my **laboratory** quickly, though I don't remember how."
"There, I mixed and drank my **formula**, half afraid it wouldn't work."

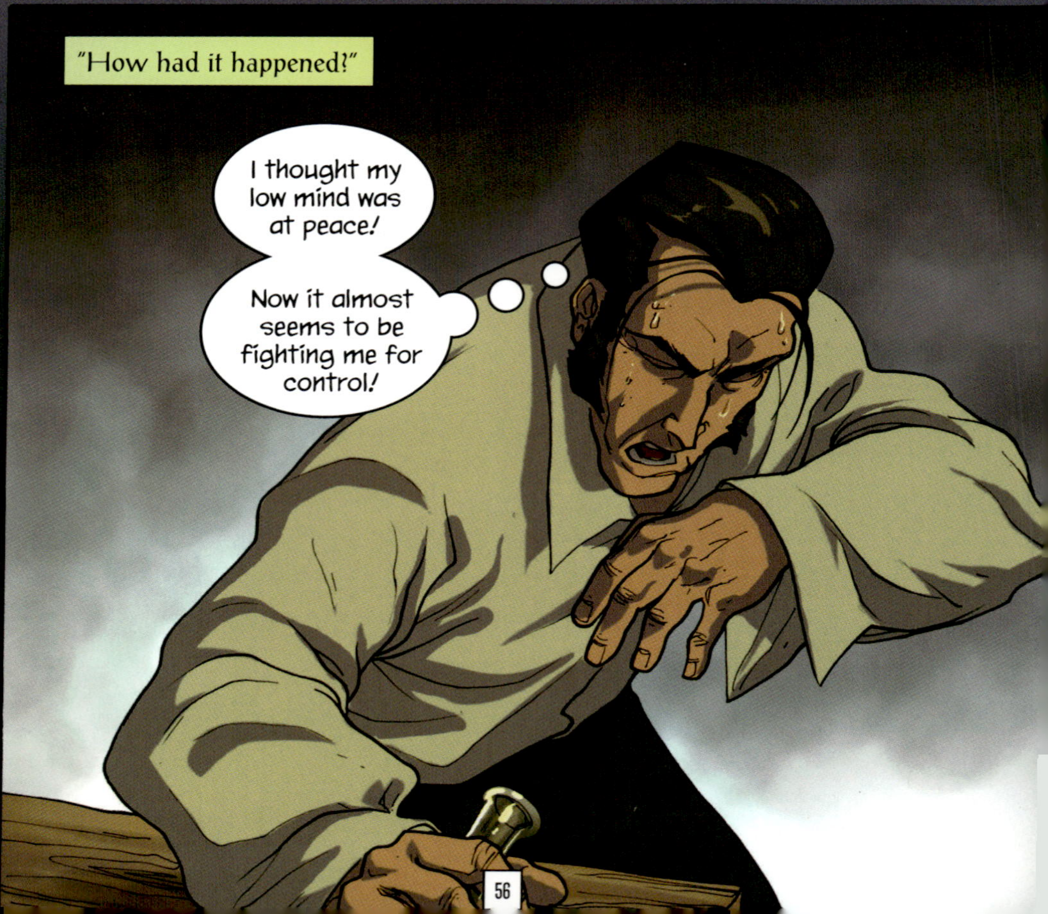
"How had it happened?"
I thought my low mind was at peace!
Now it almost seems to be fighting me for control!

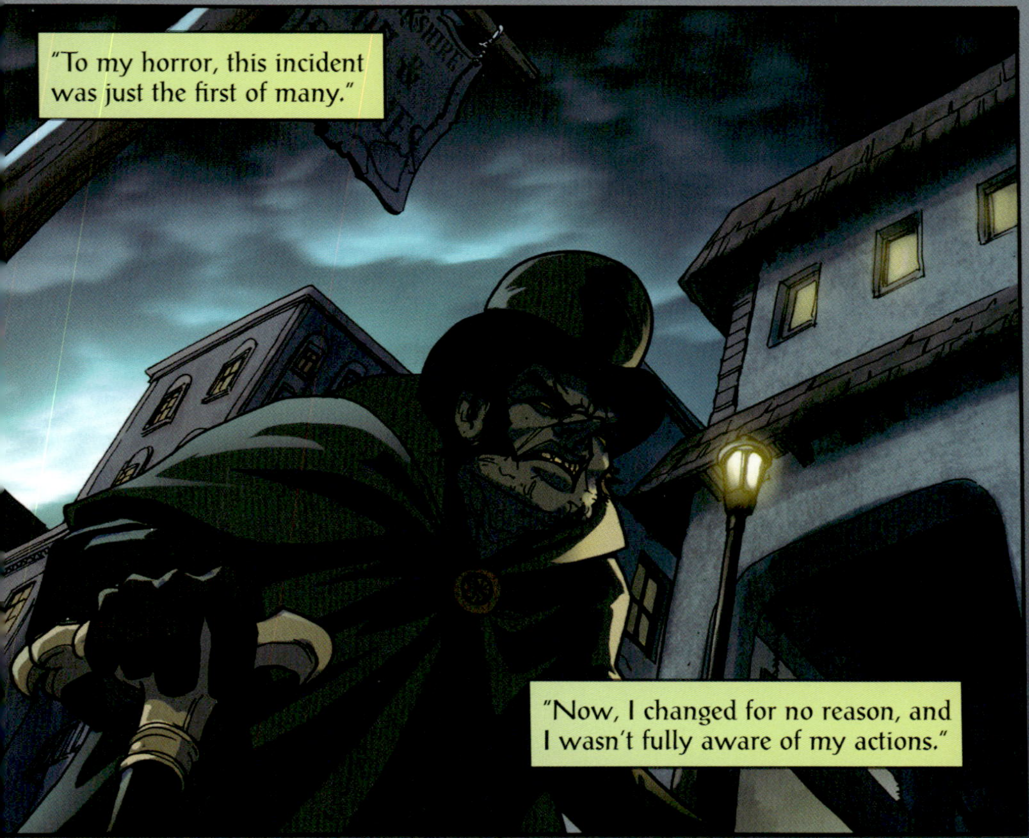
"To my horror, this incident was just the first of many."
"Now, I changed for no reason, and I wasn't fully aware of my actions."

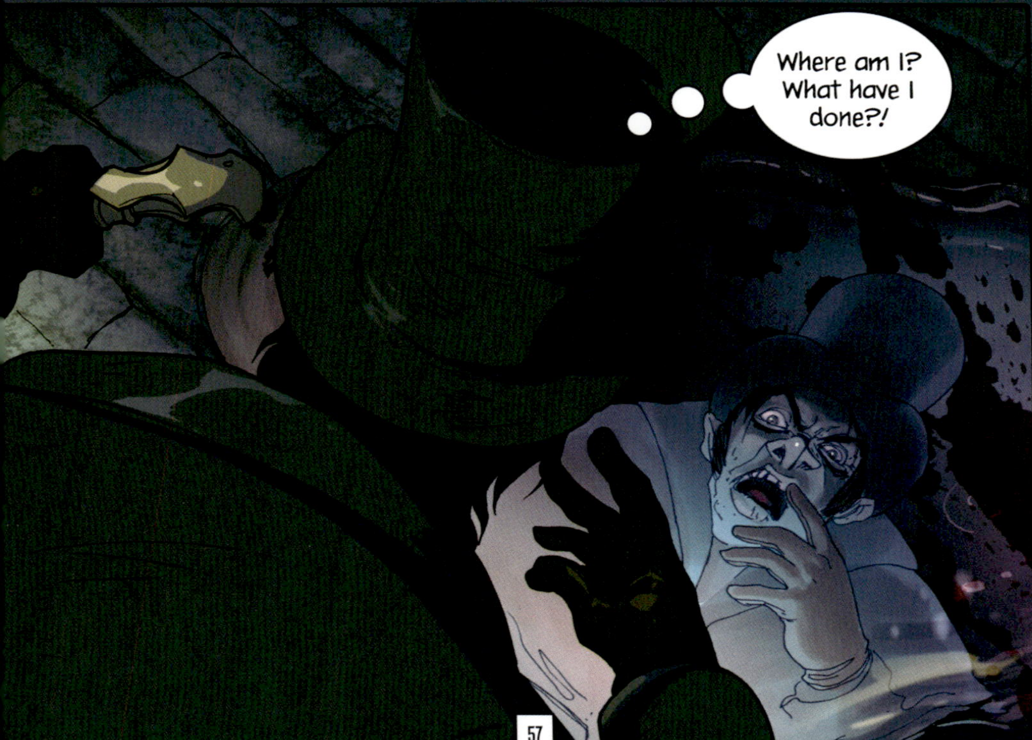
Where am I? What have I done?!

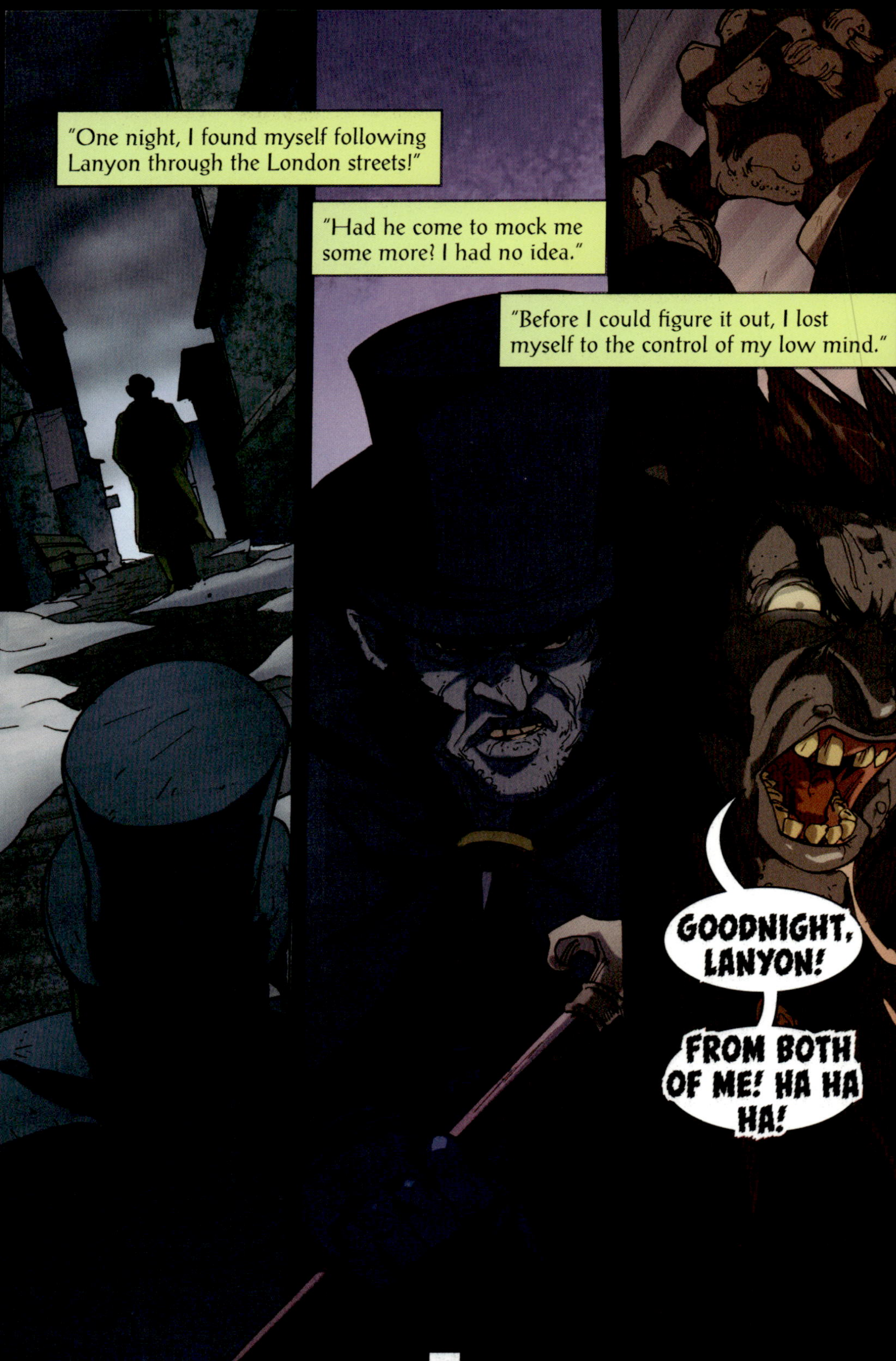
"One night, I found myself following Lanyon through the London streets!"
"Had he come to mock me some more? I had no idea."
"Before I could figure it out, I lost myself to the control of my low mind."
GOODNIGHT, LANYON!
FROM BOTH OF ME! HA HA HA!

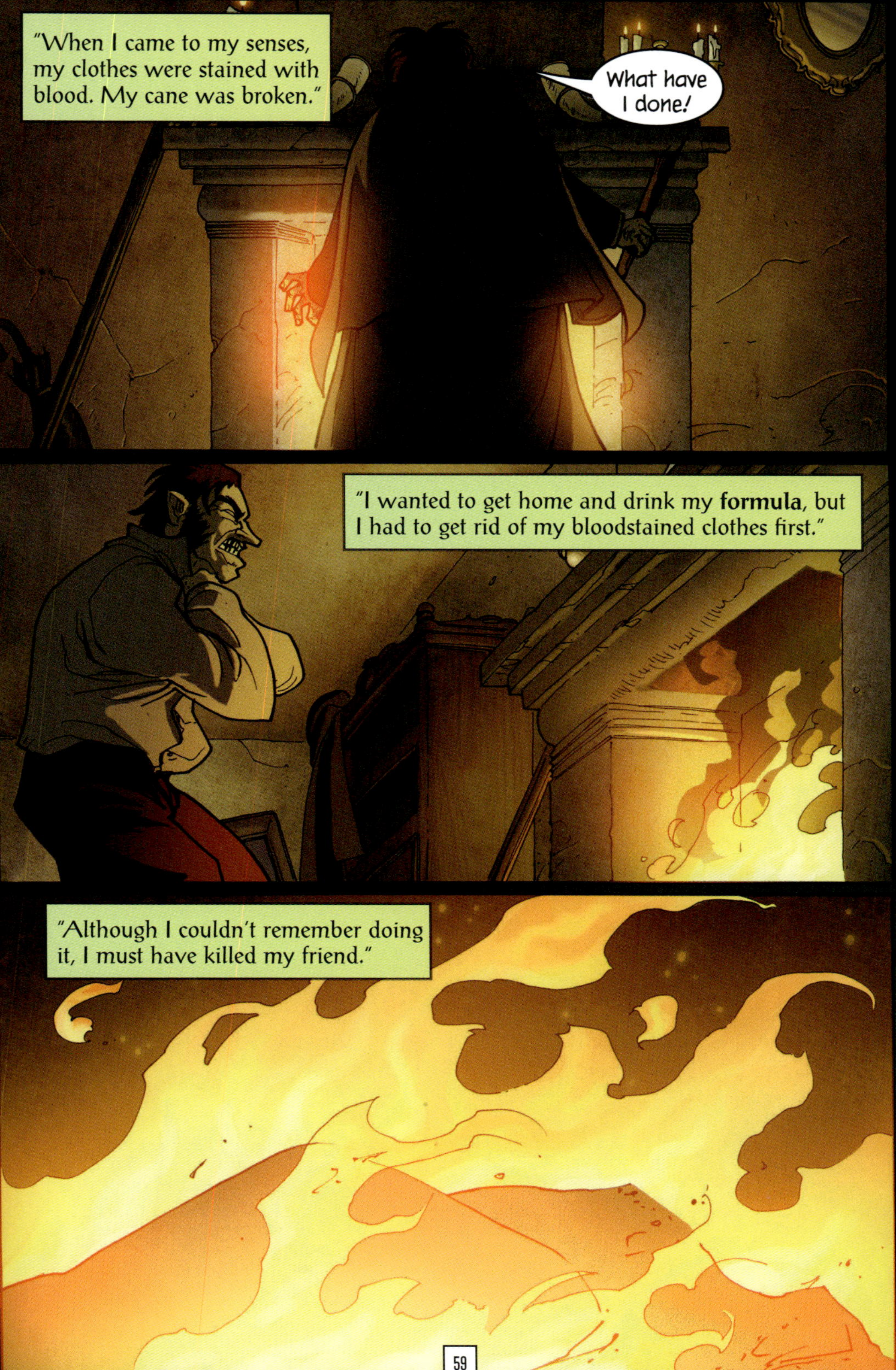
"When I came to my senses, my clothes were stained with blood. My cane was broken."
What have I done!
"I wanted to get home and drink my **formula**, but I had to get rid of my bloodstained clothes first."
"Although I couldn't remember doing it, I must have killed my friend."

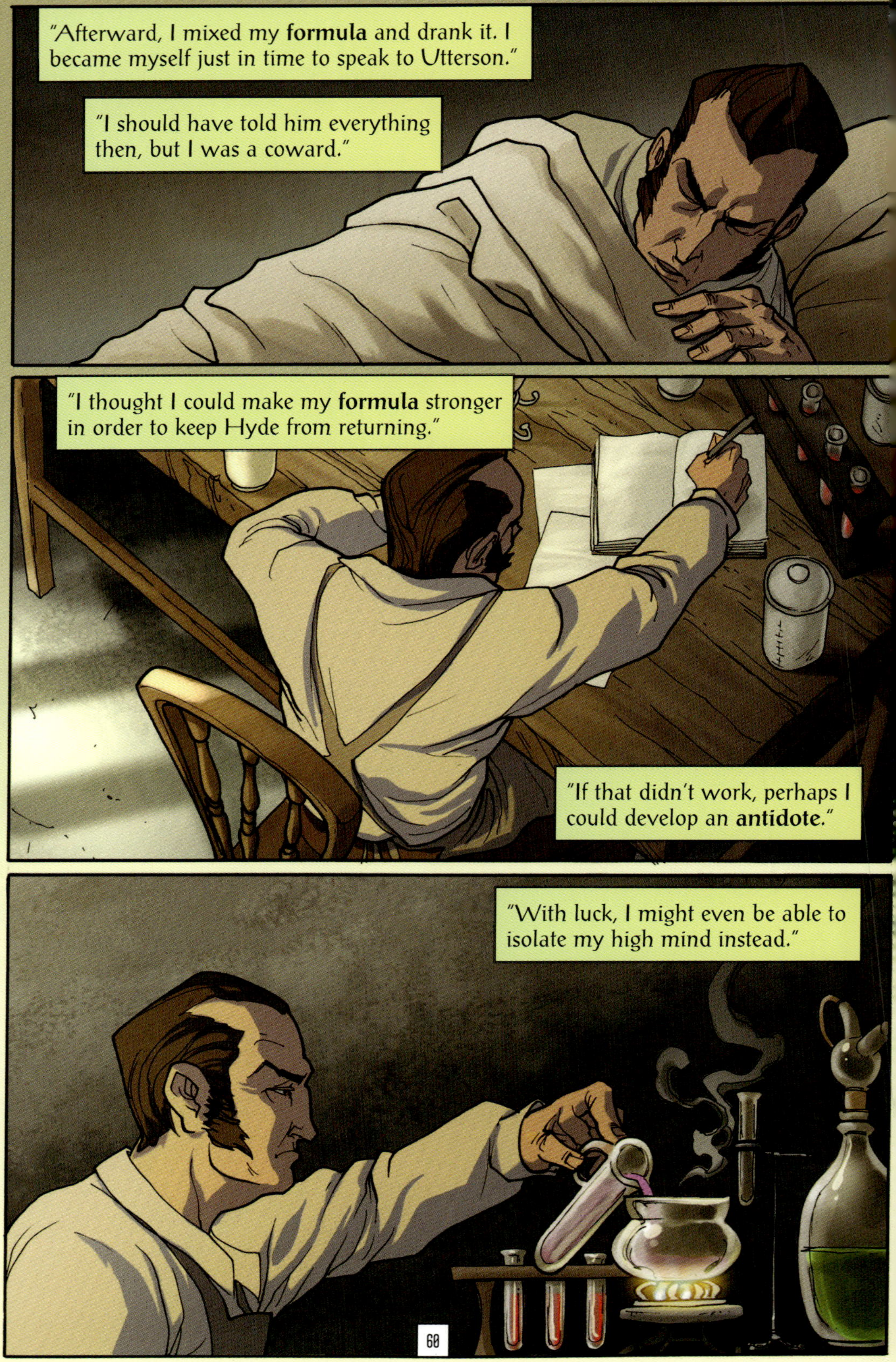
"Afterward, I mixed my **formula** and drank it. I became myself just in time to speak to Utterson."
"I should have told him everything then, but I was a coward."
"I thought I could make my **formula** stronger in order to keep Hyde from returning."
"If that didn't work, perhaps I could develop an **antidote**."
"With luck, I might even be able to isolate my high mind instead."

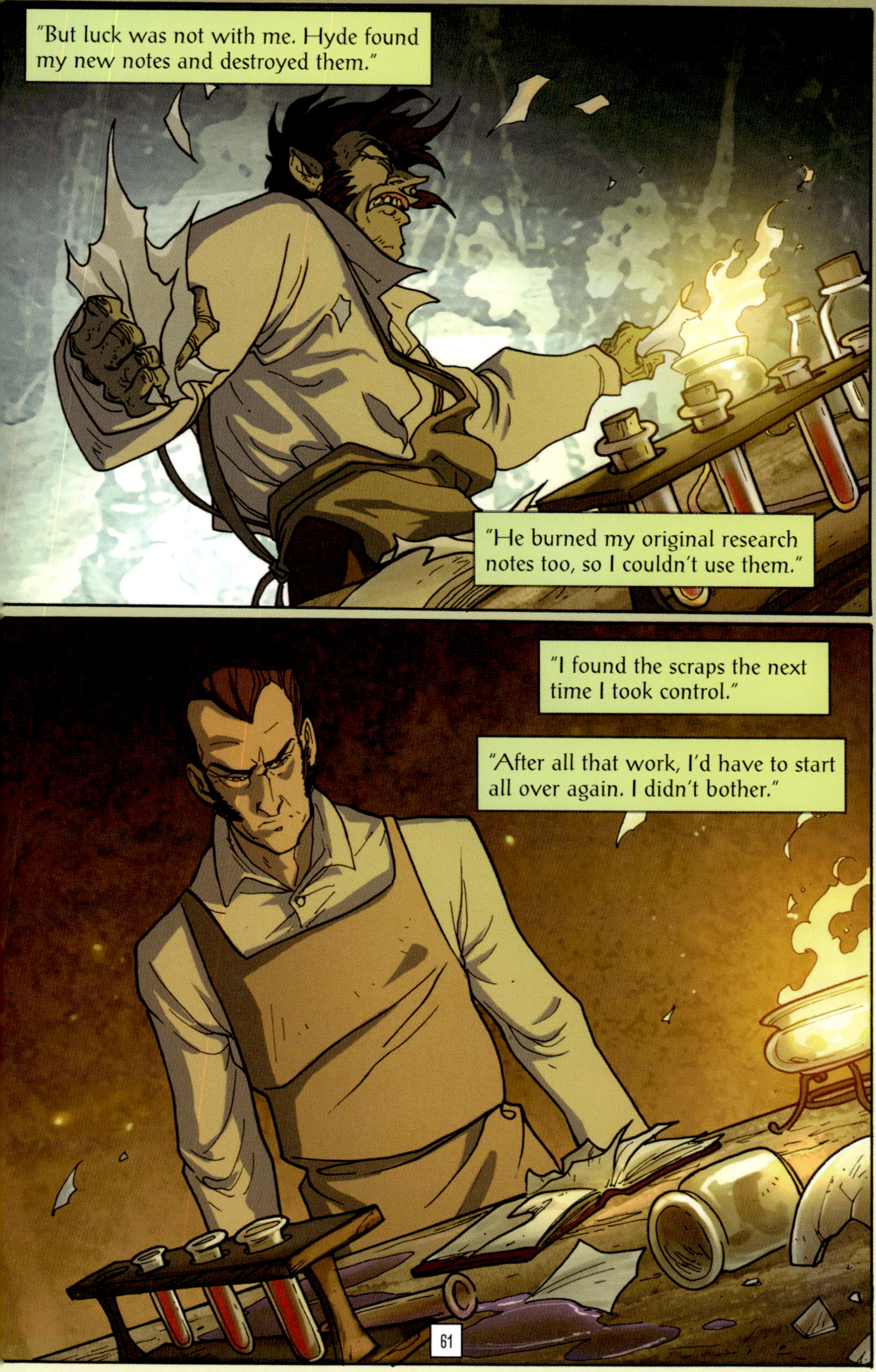
"But luck was not with me. Hyde found my new notes and destroyed them."
"He burned my original research notes too, so I couldn't use them."
"I found the scraps the next time I took control."
"After all that work, I'd have to start all over again. I didn't bother."

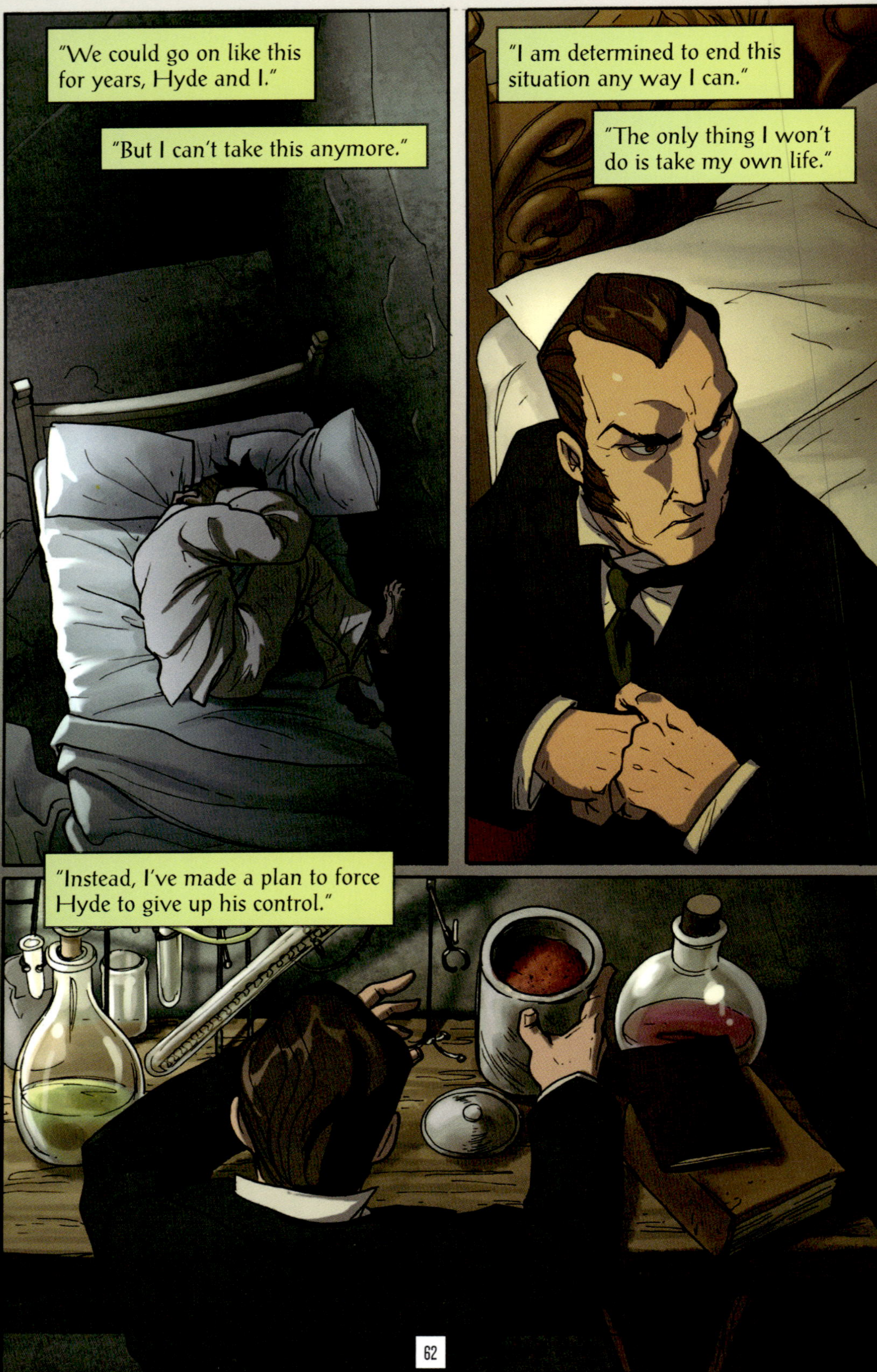
"We could go on like this for years, Hyde and I."
"But I can't take this anymore."
"I am determined to end this situation any way I can."
"The only thing I won't do is take my own life."
"Instead, I've made a plan to force Hyde to give up his control."

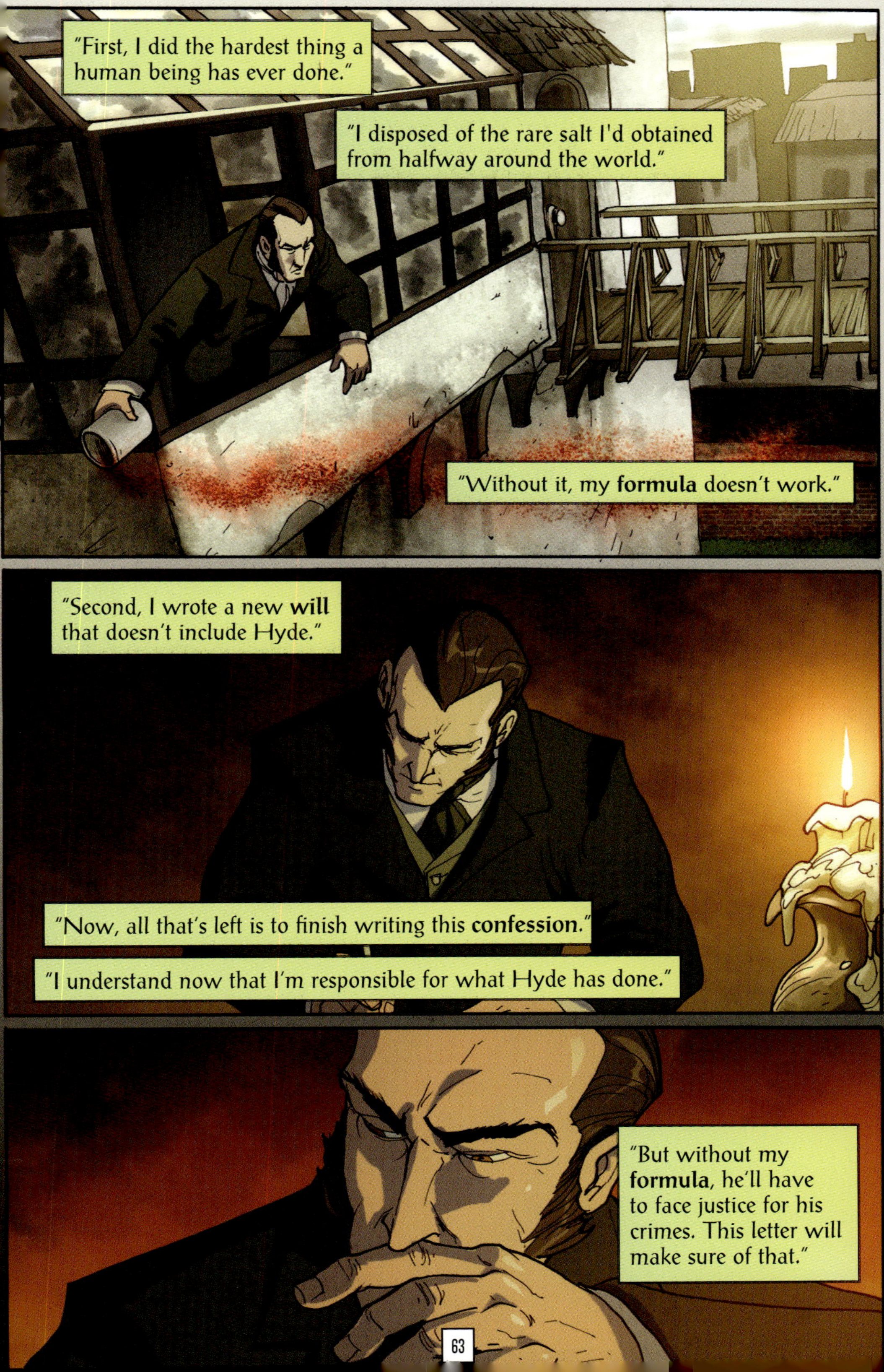
"First, I did the hardest thing a human being has ever done."
"I disposed of the rare salt I'd obtained from halfway around the world."
"Without it, my **formula** doesn't work."
"Second, I wrote a new **will** that doesn't include Hyde."
"Now, all that's left is to finish writing this **confession**."
"I understand now that I'm responsible for what Hyde has done."
"But without my **formula**, he'll have to face justice for his crimes. This letter will make sure of that."

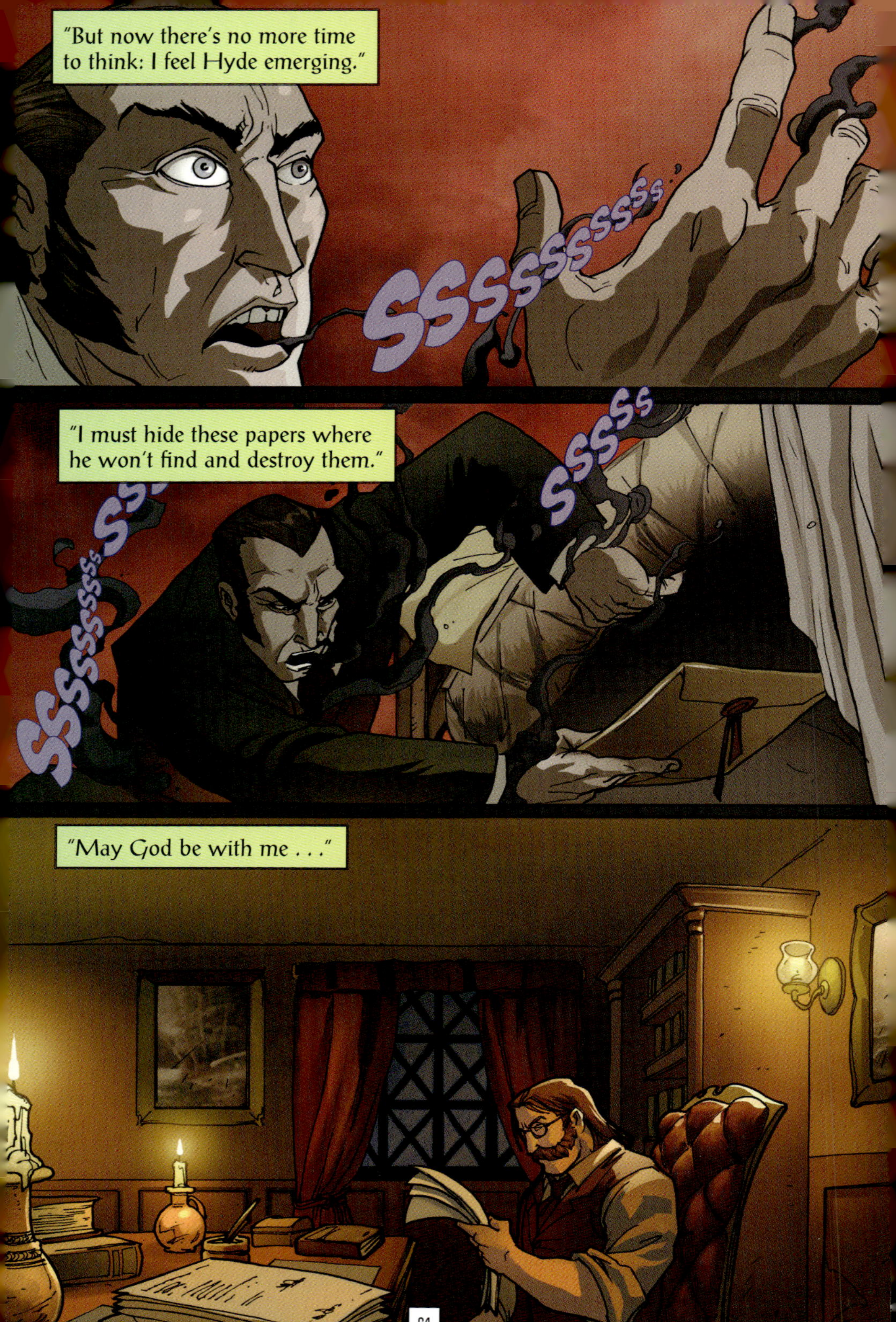
"But now there's no more time to think: I feel Hyde emerging."
"I must hide these papers where he won't find and destroy them."
"May God be with me . . ."

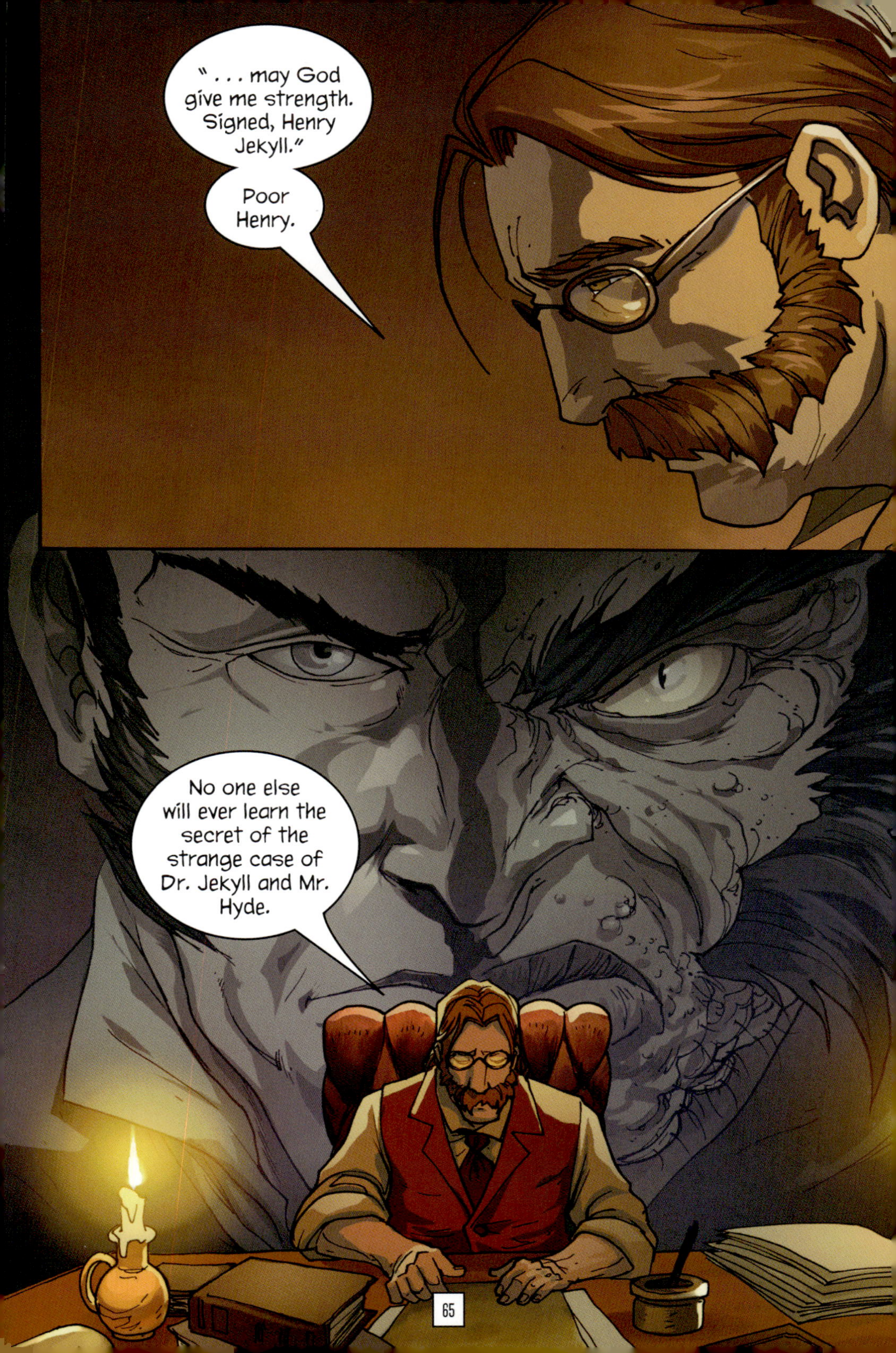
"... may God give me strength. Signed, Henry Jekyll."
Poor Henry.
No one else will ever learn the secret of the strange case of Dr. Jekyll and Mr. Hyde.

ABOUT THE RETELLING AUTHOR AND ILLUSTRATOR

Carl Bowen is a father, husband, and writer living in Lawrenceville, Georgia. He has published many novels, short stories, and comics, including retellings of *20,000 Leagues Under the Sea* (by Jules Verne), *The Strange Case of Dr. Jekyll and Mr. Hyde* (by Robert Louis Stevenson), *The Jungle Book* (by Rudyard Kipling), "Aladdin and His Wonderful Lamp" (from *A Thousand and One Nights*), *Julius Caesar* (by William Shakespeare), and *The Murders in the Rue Morgue* (by Edgar Allan Poe). Carl's recent novel, *Shadow Squadron: Elite Infantry*, earned a starred review from Kirkus Book Reviews.

Illustrator **Daniel Ferran** was born in Monterrey, Mexico, in 1977. For more than a decade, Ferran has worked as a colorist and an illustrator for comic book publishers such as Marvel, Image, Dark Horse, and Protobunker Studio.

GLOSSARY

antidote (AN-ti-dote)—something that stops a poison from working

attorney (uh-TUR-nee)—someone who draws up legal papers and helps people understand the law; an attorney is also called a "lawyer"

confession (kun-FEH-shun)—an admission of guilt for doing something wrong

experiment (ek-SPER-uh-ment)—a controlled activity carried out to discover, test, or demonstrate something

formula (FOR-myuh-luh)—a recipe for how to make a substance; the substance made using that recipe is also called a formula.

inspector (in-SPEK-tur)—someone who checks or examines things; often called a detective

laboratory (LAB-ruh-tor-ee)—a place equipped for making scientific experiments or tests

vain (VAYN)—being too proud of one's self

villain (VIL-uhn)—a wicked person

will (WIL)—a written document stating what should happen to someone's property and money when that person dies; "will" is short for "last will and testament"

COMMON CORE ALIGNED
READING QUESTIONS

1. Dr. Jekyll acts one way during the day, and a different way at night. Using details and examples from this graphic novel, describe the difference in his behaviors. *("Refer to details and examples in a text when explaining what the text says explicitly and when drawing inferences from the text.")*

2. Who is Gabriel Utterson, and how does he influence the story? *("Describe in depth a character, setting, or event in a story.")*

3. Identity is a major theme in this graphic novel. What happens in the story to make identity such an important theme? Find images and words in this book to support your answer. *("Determine a theme of a story.")*

4. Besides Dr. Jekyll and Mr. Hyde, name a character who plays a significant role in the story. What is this character's name, and why is that character significant? *("Describe in depth a character . . . drawing on specific details in the text.")*

5. This book has an exciting story. What is your favorite part of this book, and why? Again, please find images and words to support your thoughts. *("Refer to details and examples in a text when explaining what the text says explicitly and when drawing inferences from the text.")*

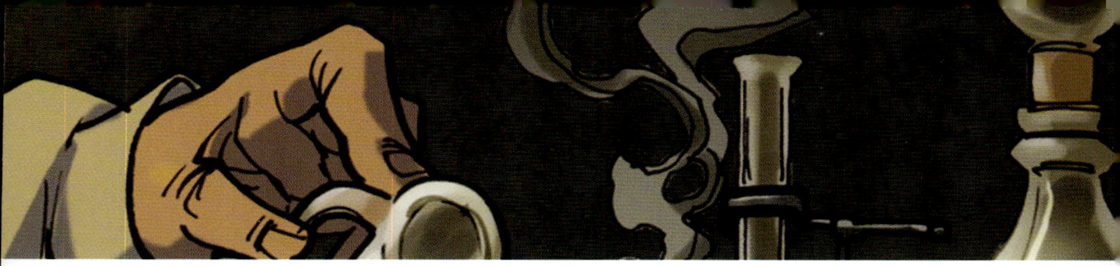

COMMON CORE ALIGNED
WRITING QUESTIONS

1. **Imagine being stuck in Dr. Jekyll's laboratory. You are hidden in a corner, and while there you witness him turn into Mr. Hyde. How would you describe the transformation to someone else after you escaped? Write a one-page profile (a detailed description of a person's character traits) of Dr. Jekyll's transformation into Mr. Hyde.** *("Draw evidence from literary . . . texts to support analysis.")*

2. **Do you think Dr. Jekyll should be held responsible for the things Mr. Hyde did? Why or why not? Explain your reasons using examples from this book.** *("Write opinion pieces on topics or texts, supporting a point of view with reasons and information.")*

3. **In Chapter 4, Mr. Hyde's bad deeds have devastating consequences, and the other characters decide they must stop him. What bad things has Mr. Hyde done up until that point? Create a bulleted list (with page number references) of the crimes Mr. Hyde has commited.** *("Write informative/explanatory texts to examine a topic and convey ideas.")*

4. **Imagine that you become a monster at night. What kind of monster would you be? Scary? Nice? Shy? Brave? Describe your monstrous self.** *("Write narratives to develop real or imagined experiences or events.")*

5. **If you could interview both Dr. Jekyll and Mr. Hyde, what kinds of questions would you ask them? Write down five questions for each character. Then predict what their answers might be based on what you know about their characters.** *("Produce clear and coherent writing in which the development and organization are appropriate to task, purpose, and audience.")*

READ THEM ALL!

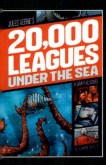

JULES VERNE'S
20,000 LEAGUES UNDER THE SEA
A GRAPHIC NOVEL
MARK TWAIN'S
THE ADVENTURES OF TOM SAWYER
A GRAPHIC NOVEL
ANNA SEWELL'S
BLACK BEAUTY
A GRAPHIC NOVEL
VICTOR HUGO'S
THE HUNCHBACK OF NOTRE DAME
A GRAPHIC NOVEL
ROBIN HOOD
A GRAPHIC NOVEL
ROBERT LOUIS STEVENSON'S
TREASURE ISLAND
A GRAPHIC NOVEL
MARY SHELLEY'S
FRANKENSTEIN
A GRAPHIC NOVEL
JULES VERNE'S
JOURNEY TO THE CENTER OF THE EARTH
A GRAPHIC NOVEL
ARTHUR CONAN DOYLE'S
THE HOUND OF THE BASKERVILLES
A GRAPHIC NOVEL
BY POWELL & FERRAN
WASHINGTON IRVING'S
THE LEGEND OF SLEEPY HOLLOW
A GRAPHIC NOVEL
BRAM STOKER'S
DRACULA
A GRAPHIC NOVEL
JONATHAN SWIFT'S
GULLIVER'S TRAVELS
A GRAPHIC NOVEL
ROBERT LOUIS STEVENSON'S
THE STRANGE CASE OF DR. JEKYLL AND MR. HYDE
A GRAPHIC NOVEL

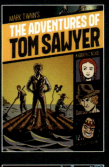

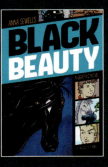

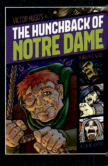

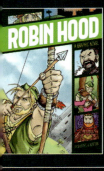

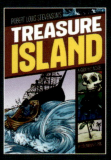

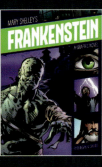

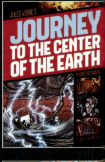

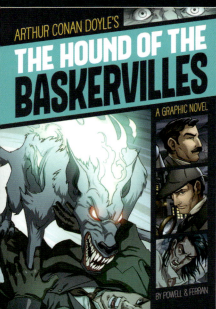

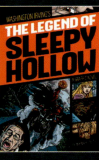

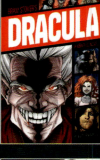

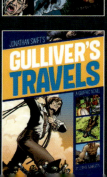

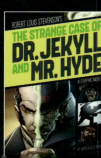

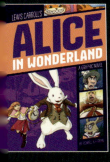

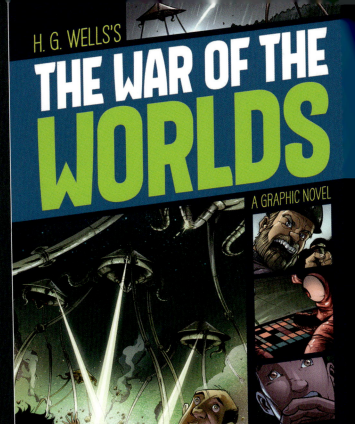

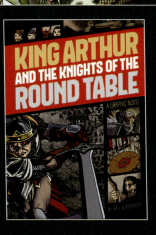